C000148973

- "*I Hate Martin Amis et al.* is a[...]
Bookworm

- "Black humor doesn't work [...]
to hollow out an empty place inside the reader. Barry does this superbly and painfully." — Michael Mcgirr, *The Saturday Age*

- "An original, compelling and darkly funny meditation on the vagaries of war, publishing, and thwarted ambition. Zorec is a monstrous creation, but one that needs to be talked about in an industry that has far more frustrated would-be geniuses than Martin Amises. That Barry has also provided a terrifying glimpse of a Balkan conflict no one seemed to understand is an added bonus." — Chris Flynn, *The Weekend Australian*

- "To say this is a somewhat unconventional novel is an under-statement. Barry plays with language in a most ingenious way, constantly toying with the reader. . . .This is the sort of literature that should be celebrated—dark, funny, and challenging—a novel that will have you revisiting certain scenes not only for reasons of clarity (this novel demands your full attention), but also for its sheer wicked inventiveness." —*Abbeys Bookshop Magazine*

- "Imagine Adrian Mole grown up, reading American Psycho, taught to shoot a Steyr SSG rifle, and sent in a bad mood to one of the most appalling of modern wars. . . . It is impressive . . . a tensely written debut novel that stings like the hell it creates." — Kate Holden, *Australian Book Review*

**Winner of the Victorian Premier's Literary Award
for an unpublished manuscript.**

Peter Barry

I Hate Martin Amis et al.

ROARING FORTIES
PRESS

Roaring Forties Press
1053 Santa Fe Avenue
Berkeley, CA 94706

Printed in the United States of America.

Library of Congress Cataloging-in-Publication Data
Barry, Peter, 1944-
I hate Martin Amis et al. / Peter Barry.
    pages cm
  "First published 2011 by Transit Lounge Publishing"--
  ISBN 978-1-938901-15-7 (pbk.) -- ISBN 978-1-938901-16-4 (kindle) --
ISBN 978-1-938901-17-1 (epub) 1. Novelists--Fiction. 2.
Snipers--Fiction. 3. Sarajevo (Bosnia and
Hercegovina)--History--Siege, 1992-1996--Fiction. I. Title.
  PR6102.A7834I43 2013
  823'.92--dc23
                                        2013005293

For Paul, Charlotte, and Richard

"I am envy.
I cannot read,
and therefore wish all books burned."
—Christopher Marlowe,
The Tragical History of Doctor Faustus

I HATE MARTIN AMIS ET AL.

In the beginning was the Word. Remember that. The word, a word, which word? It does not matter, it was a word. It was not a painting, nor was it a musical note, it was a word. And that is good enough for me.

I shall start by writing about my first victim. To start with the first, and not necessarily at the beginning, seems appropriate. The others round the campfire the other night were saying you never forget your first one, that he will always have a place in your heart—even though he has your bullet in his. (They didn't say that last bit, I just thought that up.) I suspect they're not the kind of men who willingly give way to feelings of sentimentality, yet Santo, who every time I see him asks if I've shot anyone, speaks to me as if he's concerned about my ability to cope with the situation—claiming a first victim, that is. It must be because I'm a foreigner that he worries I won't have what it takes, won't have the backbone. The rest of them, the majority, however, just treat me with suspicion, even contempt, regarding me through clouds of cigarette smoke as if I'm some phantasmagoric impostor. Why so? Surely I'm no different from the volunteers who come here from their nine-to-five jobs in other parts of the country, those who come here for fun, as if for a bit of game shooting?

And this is a game, isn't it? For me, certainly it is.

I thought they were being ironic comparing my first victim to my first lover, saying you never forget them, that they're special. They weren't being ironic, however, and although I cannot see this myself—my first victim finding a place in my heart—who am I to argue with them? They're not the kind of people you disagree with. They have what I can only describe as dead peasant stares and lugubrious eyes, and if they claim to know what they're talking about, then I shall go along with it.

He, my first one, walked into my life out of the blue, out of the silvery mist, the watery sunshine of winter, along the far bank of the River Miljacka. Even from where I was lying I could see his breath puffing in the cold morning air. He could have been smoking, but he wasn't. He was walking

4

along Snipers' Alley, which runs east–west through the city. Those who live in the apartments along this road, facing the river and exposed to the hills, have long since moved out of their front rooms and retreated to the backs of their homes.

He was wearing a corduroy jacket with leather patches at the elbows. I was surprised he wasn't wearing an overcoat—it was cold enough for one—although he did have a dark blue beret on his head. Perhaps he didn't have far to go. He could have been heading toward the university, about a mile to the west of where he was walking, but I couldn't be sure of that.

What stands out most clearly in my memory is the large pile of books he was carrying, perhaps eight or ten of them. They were cradled by his left arm, the volumes held together by a leather strap. Sometimes he'd move his right arm across to provide additional support for them, as if his left arm was becoming tired.

Now this is the interesting bit: he looked like he could be a publisher's reader, one of *them*. Or that is what I told myself. He had that air about him, of complacency and self-satisfaction, of smug superiority. That got to me. It was as if he was living on the rarefied heights of Mount Parnassus and was weary, even bored, of watching lesser mortals attempt to toil up the slopes toward him. As if he considered he had nothing left to learn in life because he already knew it all. His attitude would definitely make my task easier.

He was only four hundred yards away and there were no obstructions to speak of, just a few abandoned cars and, about halfway along the street, a burnt-out tram. My reader (note the possessive pronoun: already I have appropriated him for myself) was walking toward me from the direction of the Latin Bridge. He had, I thought, although I couldn't be certain at this distance, a faint smile on his face, glancing to the left and right as if searching for someone—but of course there was no one—on whom he could bestow a little goodwill, some munificence, his chest puffed out, looking very pleased with himself. There was a vaguely studious air about him, an air of self-absorbed dishevelment, as if he might be musing on the meaning of life. There was a bookish stoop to his shoulders, and I imagined ink stains on his fingers. This look was accentuated by a clever goatee beard and wise, owl-like glasses, the kind John Lennon used to wear. He must have been in his early fifties.

I was certain he was a reader: he looked like a bookworm. He had the walk, too; the kind of walk that says, *I'm better than you, step aside, remove yourself from my path, I am on my way to pass judgement on some lesser mortal's literary efforts.* I could spot it even from four hundred yards away. It was a busy walk, a busy reader's walk, almost gay, his steps being small and quick. I could imagine his heels going tap tap, tap tap on the pavement, as if he were important, tap tap, tap tap, impatient to get to wherever he was going. But then he wasn't going anywhere—not that he knew that yet.

I persuaded myself of all this quite quickly, in those few seconds I was watching him walk by the river, opposite my position, almost at right angles to me. He was the ideal target, made to measure, just for me: a reader, I'm sure of it. He was the kind of man who'd dismiss a manuscript with, "I feel I've read this before." He was perfect.

When I write that he was only four hundred yards away —the length of around four football pitches—it's to emphasize that he was an easy target. I could almost have shot him with my eyes closed. Although he was not that distant, he existed in a different world. He was on the inside, I was on the outside. We could have been in a theater: I was high up in the gods, in a Grbavica apartment, almost completely removed from where he was, down below in the city, on center stage. Despite that, as in any well-designed theater, we were intimately connected.

Through the telescopic sights, my reader appeared so close that I felt I could reach out and touch him. But when I lifted my head an inch, I lost him. I thought, where is he, where has he gone? And then I would spot him—but only because I knew the area in which to look. To the naked eye, he had shrunk. In the split second it had taken me to raise my eye from the sights, he had shrunk back into the anonymity of the surrounding streets and almost disappeared.

I had him in my sights again. I was in a beautiful position, propped up comfortably, the Steyr SSG steady as a rock. I tracked him along the embankment, keeping his head in the crosshair. It was so close, like a watermelon sitting on a fence at the end of a garden, it could almost have been sitting on the muzzle of the rifle. This was good, because I knew from training that the brain cavity is only six inches wide and four inches high. I imagined my shot entering his skull between the parietal and frontal bones, possibly even exiting between the parietal and occipital bones. Wouldn't it be a great shot, and a beautiful sight, if one bullet could separate the parietal, frontal, and occipital bones, so that they sprang away from the stem of the brain, leaving it exposed like the stamen of a flower? Yes, of course, it would be a physiological impossibility as well as a shooting impossibility, but hey, it was fun to imagine! I'd also welcome the opportunity to see if a reader's brain was any different from that of a normal person. It could be full of words, dust, or cobwebbed ideas. Possibly small, mean, and nasty, even vindictive. Or maybe polished and cold, like the inside of a computer: efficient, calculating, everything clicking and whirring away with frightening precision.

I could almost see the expression on his face, although, at that distance, it was beginning to blur. But he did look smug, I was sure of that. And I felt I could speak to him without even raising my voice. For a moment, I think I may have done. "I'm going to put a bullet in the middle of that head of yours, just above the ear, so that it goes straight through your pathetic brain and splashes those little grey cells all over the pavement. That's it, Mr. Publisher's Reader, let's have a look inside your head. Let's see how much is there." That's the kind of thing I might have been saying, probably trying to stop myself from freaking out, from losing my nerve.

Click, click, click. I adjusted for elevation and distance. If he was four hundred yards away and walking at, say, three miles an hour, then I had to aim a little over two body thicknesses in front of him—about thirty inches.

There were no obstructions to speak of. The once-famous poplars along the river bank had long since been felled for firewood, cut down at ground level so that now all you could see were stumps. If they had not been in such an exposed position I think the locals who are desperate for firewood would have come along and dug them up too. *Hang on a minute,* I thought, *let's have some fun with the old fool. Let's not finish this business off too fast; he's a reader after all. We don't want it to be over before it's even started. There may not be anyone else for me to shoot at for hours.*

I lowered the rifle a fraction. Through the sights, I could see the armful of books. They were bobbing about, forward and backward, upward and downward in the crosshairs. It would be a tricky shot, aiming ahead of the target, trying to time the arrival of the bullet at a certain spot with the arrival of the books. The meeting of lead with paper. I took two deep breaths. I held my breath at the end of the second exhale, just before the next inhale, squeezing the trigger, feeling the solid kick of the rifle against my shoulder. I heard the faint crack as the bullet left the barrel. A second later I inhaled.

I could have hit the strap holding the books straight on, as intended, but it was possible I'd simply knocked them out of his hands. Whichever it was, it was a good shot. His books lay around on the pavement in disarray, some shut, some open, their pages waving in the breeze, some with their spines pointing upward to the sky like miniature tents. The astonishing sight, however, was the reader on his hands and knees trying to gather up all the books I'd shot out of his arms. I could scarcely believe my eyes. There he was, inches away from being another sniper's victim, out in the open, totally exposed, and he was on all fours trying to pick up the books he'd dropped. It was so unexpected, I almost laughed. I'd taken it for granted that he'd run for cover and, in readiness for such an eventuality, had immediately ejected the spent cartridge and chambered another. I needn't have rushed. My reader, my bookish friend, was sweeping up his volumes and piling them one on top of the other with earnest enthusiasm, totally absorbed in his task, as if his very life depended on it. The man was crazy, why didn't he run for cover? I was put out. I was annoyed: did he *want* me to kill him? It was as if he was embarrassed to be put in such a predicament, Mr. Perfect being made to look a fool. I could see an old woman who must have come out of one of the apartments standing nearby, watching the reader scrabble around, like a croupier gathering and stacking chips on the roulette table. Like me, she was obviously captivated by this sight.

I bided my time, I was enjoying the show. Why wasn't he trying to hide, why didn't he take shelter? For a reader he didn't seem too clever. Could I have been mistaken about his profession? But no, on second thoughts, I was sure this is how a reader would behave in a crisis—like an imbecile. I'd envisaged firing my second shot as he ran along the pavement, bent almost double, trying to reach the safety of an apartment building. That would have made it easier.

Instead, here he was, staying put, out in the open, presenting himself as a stationary target. That wasn't much fun for me. It made it more difficult. I told myself it must be panic, he must be crapping himself. I remember reading once that a person will do anything to avoid ridicule, preferring to die rather than be shown up in front of his fellows. If it means he can prevent being made to look foolish, then he'll happily lay down his life. I've never truly believed this until that moment, but looking at the man grovelling around on the pavement gathering up his books instead of running for cover, it did look a distinct possibility.

Then the woman also got down on her hands and knees to help him pick up his books. She probably thought she was so old it didn't matter if she was shot. And to be honest I couldn't be bothered to pick her up in my scope. I was too interested in my reader. Just for a moment, however, I did wonder if she could be my long-lost grandmother—she was about the right age. I recalled my father's request: "Shoot your grandmother for me if you see her." But this was scarcely the time to settle family squabbles.

Suddenly, as if it had all become too much for him, the reader stood up, somewhat shakily, took off his John Lennon spectacles, and wiped his eyes with the back of his hand. Was he crying? Could the guardian of public taste have been reduced to tears? It appeared so. "Go on, Mr. Reader," I said out loud, "have a cry. It won't do you any good, though."

I should finish him off: he was too pathetic. He was dusting himself down in between wiping away his tears. But he still had that look about him—smugness, it was definitely smugness, as if he were saying to me, "There, you have inconvenienced me a little, you have had a little sport at my expense, but I am not fazed, I'm not going to let it get me down, I shall pick up my books and continue on my way.

Please stand aside, I have important things to do." He put his spectacles back on.

I steadied the rifle. My finger, curled around the trigger, tightened imperceptibly. At that moment a young man approached the professor and started pulling at his jacket, pointing up to the hills in my direction and speaking with great urgency. He was half bent over and he looked scared. I imagined he was trying to persuade the old buffoon to run for cover. I could almost hear what he was saying: "For heaven's sake, friend, leave your books and take shelter. Hurry! You'll get shot out here. Don't worry about your books, you can collect them later. They're only books. Your life is more valuable. Run, friend, run!"

Don't waste your breath, I muttered to myself. As my reader started to follow the young man down the street, I tracked him with the rifle. And yes, I can't explain it, but suddenly I wanted them to hurry, I wanted them out of my sight.

They'd left the old woman to pick up the books. This struck me as very ungentlemanly, although she didn't seem too unhappy or concerned by the arrangement, and continued to place one book carefully on top of another, like a librarian at the end of a hard day. She was certainly of the opinion that no one would be interested in shooting her. She was a wise old bird, certainly wiser than the reader, so I left her alone.

I left the other two alone, too. I couldn't do it. I don't know what happened, but I couldn't pull the trigger. It was harder to do than I thought. Even though I suspected one of them was a reader, I couldn't pull the trigger.

Having nothing better to do, I visited my parents. It was over Christmas and the New Year, and it was the last time I saw them before leaving England. The occasion was more memorable for John Osborne dying on Christmas Eve. He probably wasn't angry dying then, and more than happy to miss all that holiday nonsense. For the first time in his life, on his deathbed, the Angry Young Man wouldn't have been angry at all. I liked that. It was poetic. I'm certain he'd have appreciated it too.

My parents live in a nondescript Edwardian two-story house in a small town in Norfolk, on the east coast. The house is a few streets back from the promenade, so it always strikes me as being little different from living in London. When I point this out to them, my father gets angry and shouts, "What do you know! You can breathe the sea air down here. It's healthier than where you live." I can't be bothered to argue with him, so I shut up. Eventually, he quietens down, but he doesn't forget. He hoards insults—or what he perceives as insults—in the back of his head like a squirrel stores nuts in the ground. He'll sometimes take them out, often years later, dust them off, and use them as ammunition against some unsuspecting adversary who's forgotten they ever existed. In that respect he's no different from the men who sit with me around the Vraca campfire: they're brothers in bitterness. All bear grudges, all spend their days obsessing about how they can even the score.

My mother and father have always lived in the same house. My grandfather bought it when he fled from Serbia in 1940. My father was fourteen at the time, and the two of them lived there alone, rattling around in the house, with some rooms barely visited from one year to the next. My grandfather claimed he moved into the house because when he arrived in England he was going to find himself a new wife and have lots of children. Trouble is, he'd become so wary of women after the way my grandmother behaved, and so suspicious of their motives, he never married again. It was left to my father to carry on the line. He married young, to a farmer's daughter. The Wickhams had been farming in the area for hundreds of years, and weren't too happy about their only daughter marrying a foreigner. My father fell out with his father-in-law and two brothers-in-law with impressive speed (confrontation, that's his speciality), and now, if my mother wants to see any of her family, she has to sneak off and visit them secretly. After I was born, when there were four of us in the house, it was about the right size. But then my grandfather died in 1976. I was sixteen, and I missed him. He'd always spoken Serbian to me (to everyone in fact, even the bemused locals), and I think he found being with me easier than being with his own son. A few years later I left to go and live in London, to do odd jobs while I studied to be a teacher, so once again the house seemed too big for its two occupants.

The old place hasn't been painted inside or out for as long as I can remember. Around the windows the paint is peeling, and the undercoat is visible. The carpets are worn and the floorboards creak. Draughts inhabit the corridors like ghosts, and the East Anglian damp infiltrates every room, every occupant. The light shades are dimmed by a thin patina of dust, and the weak sunlight barely penetrates the lace curtains. It's a dark house, with little warmth. It could be a boarding house whose regulars have all passed away. Outside, the garden also has fallen into a state of disrepair. My father still cuts the grass, but doesn't bother to weed. "That's a woman's job," he says. "That's not for men to do." My mother obviously thought it was a man's job, because she didn't do it either.

When I was growing up, there was an open field across the road from the house. Cows grazed there, and I'd sit on the wall by our front gate and watch them, big, ungainly creatures, always chewing. I never wanted to cross the road and touch them. The cows have long since been replaced by houses, and the greenery has slowly retreated from the town like a puddle after the sun has come out. Our house is now many streets from the countryside, and my grandfather, who always said he wanted to live among trees because that's where he'd been brought up in Serbia, would be disappointed if he saw his house today.

The sea, that hasn't moved; it's still a few streets away. It's typical east coast scenery: bleak, windswept dunes with tufts of spiky grass, grey seas and low skies, and seagulls huddled together in despondent, shivering groups on the shingly beach. Only rarely can people be seen walking in the distance, and they, without exception, always have a dog with them. That's their reason for being there, the only reason anyone's ever there. In summer, an ice-cream van sometimes materializes on the promenade, the tinny music whipping across the sands toward the seagulls, like nervous pensioners in an empty ballroom waiting for someone to come and ask them to dance.

"That Milosevic is a genius. In five years he's won half of Bosnia. That's genius."

"Helped by Mladic."

"He's a genius too, no doubt about it, but his genius is on the battlefield. He couldn't have done anything without Milosevic. It's Milosevic who's pulling all the strings, even though he sits in Belgrade and tells the world he has no control over the Bosnian Serbs."

We were watching the news, Milosevic surrounded by thickset men, politicians and bodyguards—it's hard to tell the difference in this part of the world—justifying his latest incursion to the world's media. My father never watched the nightly news before the troubles started in the late eighties, after Tito's death, but now he watches it religiously. "I want to see the progress we're making." It's the only thing, apart from Manchester United, I've ever seen him show any enthusiasm for.

Soon enough he was onto his favorite hobby horse. "They tell lies, the BBC. You'd think they'd know better. They're anti-Serbian. They never mention how we've suffered."

"From the outside our point of view doesn't look too good."

"What's that supposed to mean?" He barely turned his face from the TV screen. He reminded me of an animal devouring a meal, too intent on what it was doing to spare the time to look around.

"I'm talking about the executions, the torture, the rapes, the mass graves . . . That kind of thing," I added weakly, implying there was more.

"They deserve everything they get, those bastards."

"Maybe they do. I'm just saying the BBC can't be expected to take the past into account when they may not even know about it."

"Well, they should. The Gestapo was sickened by what the Ustase did to us during the Second World War—even the Gestapo. Imagine that! They weren't exactly a bunch of innocents. Do you know what the Ustase and the Croat death squads did to us?"

And even though I answered yes, he went on to describe the atrocities to me for the hundredth time.

"Some of the men presented one of their officers with a bucketful of eyeballs—Serbs' eyeballs. What do you think of that?" He tapped my forearm forcefully with a finger. "And what was Croatia's reward for committing such atrocities? They were given Bosnia, that's what. That was their reward for their barbarity and for killing one and a half million of our people." And he threw himself back into his chair as if there might be a Croatian crouching there behind him and he was intent on squashing the life out of him.

My mother sighed. It was usually the sign she'd heard something she disapproved of, but the only reaction it ever got from my father was a look of scorn. My mother didn't understand the situation in Yugoslavia, and didn't want to. She reacted in the same way to the conflict in Northern Ireland. "I don't see why people can't get on with each other."

Sometimes I tried to explain the political, religious. and racial issues at the heart of the problem. "It's quite simple," I'd say to her. "There are Christians, Jews, and Muslims, and then there are social democrats, communists, and liberals. You also have Serbs, Croats, and Bosnians, Macedonians and Montenegrins, Hungarians and Albanians, plus a few Slovenes, and they all hate each other. Every group hates every other group, Mum, and every person in every group is trying to kill every person in every other group. That's all you have to remember. It's really quite simple."

"I see," she said, not seeing at all, the expression on her face as if she'd just been given ten seconds by God to explain the meaning of life and she didn't quite know where to begin. "But I still don't see why it should stop them being friends with each other. I think it's un-Christian, carrying on the way they do."

My father always said to me: "She's a good woman, your mother, but like a lot of her sex she's stupid." Coming from a man who's never read a book in his life, criticizing someone who is never without a book in her hands, this argument was scarcely persuasive to me. "She doesn't know anything unless it's to do with housework. That's all she has room for in that head of hers—housework." His other damning indictment of his wife of almost forty years was: "She's a farmer's daughter, so what can you expect?" Which was a little rich from a man whose father had been little more than a Serbian peasant.

I said to him now, just to niggle him, "You've told me that before, about the eyeballs."

"Well, did I tell you about the massacre at Celibici?" he demanded, leaping forward fifty-odd years to bolster his argument.

I dismissed the massacre with a flick of my hand. "All I'm saying is that the media has to come up with good guys and bad guys. It makes every situation easier to understand. It sells more newspapers if there are good guys and bad guys. The public can grasp that; it's nice and simple. They like to have someone to hate, that's what you don't seem to understand."

"Don't tell me I don't understand. It's you who doesn't understand." Pointing his finger at me: "You know nothing about Serbia. It's in your bones, and yet you're ignorant of our history."

My father has been angry all his life. He stared at me blankly before turning back to the screen, back to devouring the news. If he's not watching the progress of the war on television, he's reading about it in the newspapers. He's an addict. At the shop he prefers to read newspapers than to talk to his customers. Sometimes I wonder how he keeps any of them. "Morning, Mr. Zorec," they'll say, or "Morning, Pavle," and he'll grunt from behind the counter, barely lifting his face out of the bowl of black print. If there were another newsagency in the town, I think they'd all leave him. But there isn't.

I was annoyed by his accusing me of not understanding the history of his motherland. He'd explained it to me often enough, and I'd also read many books on the subject. I knew, for instance, that if you asked an Englishman to name his enemy in the Second World War, he'd answer, the

Germans. There were others, but basically it was the Germans. In Yugoslavia it was nowhere near as simple.

There was a war between Germany and Italy on one side and the Yugoslav state on the other, another between those two countries and numerous resistance movements, another between the Croatians and the Serbs, and a fourth between Tito's communist partisans and Draza Mihajlovic's royalist Chetniks. Now that's what I call a proper war; messy, bitty, not at all clear-cut, anarchic—a Balkanized war.

The great thing about all these twists and turns in Yugoslavia's history, these collaborations and betrayals, this switching from friend to foe overnight, is that it gave future generations the justification for every outrage any of them wanted to commit, ever. "But we only did that because you once . . ." And it's always been that way. Not just during the Second World War, but since the Romans first invaded and conquered the region, right up until Tito somehow managed to hold the place together for thirty or forty years. As soon as he died, along came the Yugoslav wars of the 1990s, which are still going strong, luckily for me.

In the Balkans they do everything on a big scale. Why make do with just one enemy when you can have a whole lot of them? Why not do away with sides completely and have absolutely everyone fight absolutely everyone else, a complete free-for-all? There's none of this Christian hypocrisy about loving your neighbor in this part of the world. These people are honest: they face up to reality, to the fact that everyone hates their neighbors. There's no pretence, no turning of the other cheek. They're not like Londoners, waiting for the middle of the night before skulking around to cut a branch from a neighbor's tree or poison his dog or set fire to his garden shed. They're out there in broad daylight, doing it while the neighbor and his wife and little kiddies are pressing their disbelieving, gaw-ping, tear-streaked faces up against the windows, watch-ing. Now that's healthy.

One thing that is clear to me is that this war, or these wars, right now won't resolve anything. The fighting will start up again soon after peace has been declared, and it'll continue. It'll continue forever because the causes are too deep-rooted and because too many people are having a good time.

When the news was finished my father said, as if it should be patently obvious to everyone, "Muslims should live in a Muslim country and Serbs in a Serb country and they should never be forced to mix. Peoples of different nationalities can't live together, that's the truth of it."

My mother, as always, was sitting in the corner of the room, reading, keeping a weather eye on the flickering im-age in the opposite corner as if one day she hoped it might throw up something that would be of interest to her. It was an extremely rare occurrence, although she never ceased to be optimistic.

"Do you think Sarajevo will fall soon?" I asked. The ini-tial approach had to be made. He had to be seduced, made to feel that a supplicant was eagerly requesting his opinion on some matter or other.

"The scum can't hold out much longer. Then we'll have the whole city. He's a genius, that man, an absolute genius." A minute later he turned away from the television and looked at me. "We were going to be happy with half of the city once, but not now, not now they've dug their heels in and are refusing to give us anything. Now they'll get what's coming to them—nothing at all."

My mother continued to read, her face expressionless, her thoughts as secretive as my father's were open. She knew better than to open her mouth. Later he said (and this is the important bit), "I wish I was younger. I'd be over there in a shot."

"What for?"

"To share in the victory, that's what's for. To march into Sarajevo when it falls. To stick it up those bastards who made us suffer so much in the past. Nothing would give me more pleasure than to shoot a few of those animals, and trample their brains in the mud." My mother sighed. "Fact is, I don't believe they have any brains, so it would be difficult to do." He laughed, a low, almost snorting laugh, a laugh of anger.

"They don't need you out there. They don't need anyone. They're doing fine without help from outside."

"So how come they've got mercenaries fighting for them? Mladic has mercenaries in his army. If he has no need of anyone, why are they there?"

"Has he?"

"They need all the help they can get, especially now the whole world is turning against us. The UN is taking Bosnia's side, so is NATO. It becomes more obvious every day. They talk about food aid and about not becoming involved, but they're shooting our men all the time they're saying it. They're not neutral."

"The UN?"

"No one else. There have been reports recently of Mladic's men coming under fire. The UN is changing from being peacekeepers to active participants."

"That's because we continue to invade the so-called safe areas. The UN probably gets a little upset about that. Their job is to keep the safe areas safe."

I was always aware when I spoke to my father of feeling constricted, as if there were something in my throat. It was hard to breathe, almost like he was intent on suffocating me. I'd hold back, sensing that I couldn't be myself. Why that should be so now, after all these years, I don't know. There's nothing unconstrained about our relationship, no spontaneity. It's like two people manacled against opposing walls, gagged, bound hand and foot, trying to communicate. He's the same with my mother. Without fail she goes along with whatever he says. That's why she married him, she told me once, because he was so insistent. I suspect she also married him to escape her family. She was a dreamer, and a foreigner must have seemed romantic back then. He's definitely always got his own way. Even when he told her one child was enough, she didn't object.

"And why shouldn't we invade the safe areas?" My father had at last turned away from the screen and was now leaning on the arm of the chair, his chin pushed aggressively forward as if confronting a complete stranger in the pub, not his own son in the sitting room. His knuckles were white above the black curly hairs on the backs of his fingers, a vein on the side of his temple looked, to me at any rate, aggressively prominent, and he was clenching and unclenching his jaw with alarming rapidity. "What you call safe areas belong to us anyway. How can you invade your own home, answer me that? How can you invade your own home?" He'd lapsed into Serbian, something he always did when he got excited.

"I'm not saying we shouldn't. It's just that the UN won't see it like that. I'm playing devil's advocate, that's all."

He fell back into his armchair, more conciliatory, trying to make me understand. Age had softened him a little, but not much. "We must get what we can as quickly as possible. The UN will turn on us eventually. Look at NATO. Just carried out the biggest air raid in their history on our positions in Krajina. And it's going to get worse. They know they have to do something. We have to hurry."

I still don't know if my father was trying to put the idea in my head, or if such a thought had never struck him. But that's exactly what he did, just before the New Year, he put the idea into my head.

In March, the night before I left for Sarajevo, I phoned home to say good-bye. My mother couldn't speak; she simply cried down the phone. At one point she managed to sob, "I'm praying to God to keep you safe." My father didn't tell me to keep safe or wish me well, all he said was: "Shoot your grandmother for me if you see her."

I heard my mother in the background. "Pavle, don't say such things."

"She deserves it," he answered, half to my mother, half down the phone, "walking out on me like that. She wasn't a mother."

"How old would she be now?" I asked.

"When your grandfather and I left Serbia in 1940, she was thirty-four or thirty-five. So that would make her eighty-nine or ninety."

"Do you know where she's living?"

"No idea. If the bitch is still alive, she'll be in Sarajevo. So shoot any old woman you see. If we're lucky, it will be my mother." He laughed down the phone.

When my grandfather fled from the Ustase atrocities, he took my father with him. That was why he left the country, to save his son's life. But his wife, my grandmother, refused to accompany him. She didn't want to leave her homeland. My grandfather never forgave her for what he considered to be this act of betrayal, and for the remaining thirty-six years of his life he would talk about "the perfidy of women!" His English was never good, so I don't know where he got that word from, but he used it all the time, whenever any woman displeased him. He lumped every member of the so-called fair sex together. I've heard my father use the same expression about my mother: "Oh the perfidy of women!"

I left for Sarajevo in early March. No one saw me off, but that didn't bother me. It gave me time to visit the airport bookshop for a quick sneer, a quiet scoff, a quizzical snigger. I wasn't disappointed. The shelves were full of dross, of clichéd, unimaginative, unadulterated garbage—and that was me being generous. I could tell from the covers what the books were like inside. They should have been pulped at birth. At the very least they should have carried stickers saying, "Warning: junk. Reading this book could seriously damage your health," and shown lurid, livid photographs of a tumorous brain or a purulent, cataracted eye. Yet these novels were published, that's what had me staring open mouthed with wonder at their doorstop bulk, their embossed, gold- and-silver-lettered covers.

I had to leave the shop before I vomited. I rushed for the exit, doubtless green and perspiring like some hyperactive Martian when—and I swear I could almost hear the heavenly music and see a choir of angels descend—I saw on an island display all of its very own, like a diamond rising from a sea of dung, Martin Amis's new novel, *The Information*. I stopped dead. A pure, blinding light flooded that sanctified spot, and I suddenly felt like a plane rising above the clouds into an arctic, tropospheric wonder of brilliant sunshine and cobalt blue. Everything slowed. Everyone parted before me as I drifted, almost weightless, toward the inspired exhibit. I reached out . . .

Crashing back through the sound barrier to earth, to humdrum, noisy reality, I thrust the book at the assistant behind the counter. There was only a hardback edition, which for me was a real extravagance, but I knew there wouldn't be a paperback out for months. "Excuse me," I said politely, attempting to give the bookshop management the benefit of the doubt. "I believe there's been a mistake."

"Eh?" The mindless girl could barely look at me.

"You shouldn't be stocking this. It's scarcely appropriate for your shelves."

"Excuse me?" she snapped, taking the book out of my hands and studying the cover with a furrowed brow. Enlightenment was obviously not forthcoming. "What you want, sir? We're very busy."

"It's a literary work," I explained, trying to remain patient. "*Lit-er-ary*. It's not an airport book, not junk. I suggest you remove it from your shelves before your customers become upset."

Some tight-arsed businessman behind me, clutching his Samsonite-executive-international-traveler-suitcase-cum-wardrobe-on-wheels with one hand and a fat novel with a scantily clad, breast-thrusting demoiselle on a blasted moor in the other, tutted impatiently behind me. He was attempting to signal to me, like I was some paddleboat on the Serpentine, that my time was up and I should now move out of the way and give someone else a go with the assistant. I turned and gave him a withering look, daring him to tut one more time.

"I dunno anything about that," the girl said. "You can talk to the manager if you want."

Despairing of ever starting a meaningful dialogue with the single brain cell buried deep within the empty, echoing caverns of the creature's cranium, I bought the novel and went to sit in the departure lounge. I tried to find a seat away from everyone else, but without success, so I was obliged to study my fellow passengers, whose unreality surprised me. It shouldn't have. I decided long ago that people at airports are definitely not real. They're in a state of limbo, either leaving or arriving, but never present. And they do everything—walk around, sit down, slap their children—as if conscious of being observed. Which, of course, they are—by me. Ready to put them down in my notebook.

Later, as we climbed steeply over the city, I peered down at the streets and houses as the rain-heavy clouds settled over them—the dull and leaden sky covering so many dull and leaden lives. I felt relief at escaping. It would be a change. I hadn't had a holiday for years. It would be a laugh, with a spot of shooting thrown in on the side.

I found it difficult to concentrate on reading, although I did notice, rifling through a few pages of *The Information*, the signatory word play and brilliantly self-aware writing. Overcome by a discomforting mix of envy, awe, and airline food, I put the book to one side and contented myself with staring out of the window at the snow-covered countryside below. Everything was white, except for the blackness of the forests and woods. There was a starkness and simplicity about the landscape that made me feel I was looking down on a series of giant Dürer woodcuts.

A minibus was waiting for me at Belgrade airport. Four passengers were already on board: volunteers who'd just flown in from Germany. They greeted me with silent stares and an unsmiling indifference that bordered on hostility. They were fridge-like, so tall and wide I was reminded of the sailing ship in the bottle trick, and wondered how the driver had squeezed them all into his vehicle. No one spoke on our journey to Pale. The town, situated up in the mountains about ten miles southeast of Sarajevo, is the Serb seat of government in Bosnia and the place from which the siege is directed. The narrow cobbled streets were a chaos of rushing, shouting officials, army trucks, and a few sour-faced locals. We were told this level of activity in Pale was unusual, and due to Mladic meeting with Serbia's military and political leaders to discuss their endgame. I immediately worried that they were about to sign a peace treaty.

About twenty of us, many of whom I guessed were from within Yugoslavia, had lunch in a deserted school hall. A plate of five different kinds of meat and one vegetable—raw onions—was put down in front of us. The only bread on the table was salted. Those around me ripped into the meat like animals—or maybe just Serbians? I was the only person who didn't look too enthusiastic about the fare. After lunch we were kitted out, briefed, signed some declaration of loyalty to the people of Serbia, and then provided with a Steyr SSG. When they put the rifle in my hands, I felt nothing. I was surprised. I somehow thought this would be a defining moment in my life, that I'd feel like a new man or something, but I didn't. It was disappointing. I wondered if I'd feel so indifferent if I shot someone.

We spent the night in temporary barracks, and the next morning were driven in the back of an army truck to a cold, windswept ridge about one thousand feet above Sarajevo.

On one side of the Pale road, overlooking the suburb of Grbavica, lies the Vraca memorial park, dedicated to the partisan liberators of Sarajevo in the Second World War. An official with a clipboard informed us, as we climbed down from the truck, that it was from this hill, in 1945, that the campaign to win back the city was started. I think he was trying to make a point.

Our camp, along with a handful of houses and a scattering of small trees and bushes, is on the other side of the Pale road, nestled in a hollow beneath the summit of Mount Trebevic and hidden from the town to the north. Higher up the mountain, near the summit, is a forest.

Every now and again I heard a deep and distant boom. I knew this was gunfire, but no more than that. Now I was excited.

I met Santo as soon as I stepped down from the army truck. He told me he shouldn't even have been in camp that day, so I was lucky to meet him. That was how he put it to me later: "You were lucky to meet me." He was laughing as he said it, but I could see he meant it. He shook hands with all the new arrivals, shouting "Welcome!" many times and slapping everyone on the back, but he adopted me. "I saw you had a book in your hands when you arrived in the village, so I knew you were intelligent. I am tired of stupid people. Anyway, I do not like Germans, even when they come and fight for us, and fellow Yugoslavs do not interest me. But an Englishman, that is different. You are the eccentrics of the world." He finished this tortuous, rapidly spoken welcome by asking: "What are you reading?"

"It's a novel I picked up at the airport."

He grabbed the book from my hand. "Martin Amis? He is English, I suppose." I nodded. "I do not read novels, I do not like them," he said, dismissing the millions of books since *Pamela* with great decisiveness. "Already my life is exciting enough." He thrust it back into my hands. I didn't bother to say anything, but wondered if he was any different from the stupid people he'd just mentioned.

"Follow me." He walked off. I looked across to where the others who'd accompanied me from Pale were being addressed by the official with the clipboard. "Shouldn't I speak to him?" I called after Santo. He stopped. "You want to live in a tent or a house this winter? If you talk to him, you will live in a tent." I followed him. "No one cares where you stay or what you do," he said as we left the road and trudged across what could have been either a snow-covered field or a garden. "We are an easygoing people." If Serbs are easygoing, I thought, what does that make everyone else?

We climbed over collapsed fences and a semidemolished wall, and walked past houses that had once belonged to Muslims and Croats before they were expelled by the Serbs. There was no one to be seen anywhere. Some of the houses had obviously been shops once upon a time; now their windows were smashed and their contents looted. Most had been stripped bare. In a few I could see makeshift beds and tables, and the glow of bare light bulbs. The novel-hater disappeared through a doorway, and I followed. It was a square room with a dirt floor. Against the walls were four bunks. There was one small table and a chair that scarcely looked strong enough to sit on—nothing else. I had an unpleasant sense of déjà vu, my London prison cell of a few months earlier coming suddenly to mind. Santo took my bag and threw it onto one of the beds. "You can sleep there. There are three of us in here, but this bed is free. It belonged to a man who was killed. You are lucky, my friend. That is the only reason you are living in a house and not a tent—because he is dead. I will tell Papo you are here."

We left the house and walked farther from the memorial park until we came to a camp. There were around twenty small tents scattered among the trees. I saw some of the new recruits being allocated tents. I realized there had to be others elsewhere in the memorial park, and Santo later told me there were temporary camps like this one all the way around the city, up in the hills. "But you will make this camp your home, the same as me."

In front of the tents was an open space with a fire. Santo said that it was kept going all day and night, although during daylight hours it was only embers. Around the fire was an assortment of seats, blocks of cement, wooden boxes, barrels, and logs that had been spared the flames. On one side of the clearing, farthest from the houses, at the edge of what appeared to be a small wood but could have been a forest, was an enormous pile of firewood. Apart from the new recruits moving into their tents, there were few people to be seen. It was like a school corridor during class time.

Santo led me to a long, prefabricated hut at the western end of the open space, which turned out to be the camp kitchen. Inside were a half-dozen dubious-looking individuals, peasants with stubborn, sly faces who looked like they'd long ago worked out how to get the better of every situation or person they ran into. They had a duplicitous, calculating look, as if they were weighing up the odds just as they weighed up the potatoes and meat they were now preparing for the evening meal. They eyed me suspiciously as one of their number started making the two cups of coffee requested by Santo.

While we waited, my self-elected friend leant over the counter and peered into a vast saucepan. "Hey, is this what we're eating this evening?" he shouted.

"It is," replied the large individual preparing our coffees.

"What is it?"

"You know what it is, Santo."

"Tell me what it is, fat man."

"It's stew," and I could see the rolls of stubbled fat beneath the kitchen hand's chin start to wobble with mirth. I wondered if he found his stew funny, or Santo.

"It's stew, is it?"

"That's what I said."

"But we had stew last night, and the night before that, and the night before that. We've had stew every night I can remember."

The men in the kitchen were now grinning—in a leering fashion. "That's the truth of it," said the fat man.

"So why don't you cook something else? Why don't you give us a choice, you unshaven pig?"

"You do have a choice, you fucking rat bag."

"I have a choice, do I?" Eyeballing his adversary across the steaming saucepan.

"You do. You can fucking take it, you son of a city whore, or you can fucking leave it."

The men behind the counter laughed. Not in the least fazed, Santo laughed also.

We took our coffees and went and sat by the campfire. He told me how his home had once been in the city to which he was now laying siege.

"I am fighting to return home. My wife and boy are now in Belgrade. Look." He produced the soldier's obligatory creased photograph from inside his army coat. "He's nine. Happily, he is too young to fight in this war. He will be able to study and get himself a good job when he is older. I love him to death."

"And your wife?"

"I do not love her to death. She is a bitch. It is better that she is not around—more peaceful."

At that moment a man shuffled across the grass toward where we were sitting. Despite the cold he was wearing only a pair of trousers and an open shirt. His huge stomach was covered in thick black hair, which he scratched with one hand. In his other hand there was a bottle from which he took regular sips, like a baby at the breast who wants the reassurance of knowing his source of comfort hasn't gone away. He hadn't shaved for days. His face drooped—everything drooped, the bags beneath his eyes, his jowls and chin, his shoulders and chest, and, most noticeable of all, his stomach. I guessed that he'd just got out of bed and was suffering from a serious hangover. He and Santo talked briefly, the man staring rudely at me, but saying nothing. He half raised one leg and let out a fart. Without further comment, he shuffled back where he came from.

"He's going to work now," said Santo.

"To work?"

"Yes. To snipe."

I wondered how he would be able to set his sights. As if reading my thoughts, Santo said, "Everyone is drunk when they shoot. You will be too. It is easier."

After our coffee, we walked back to the Vraca memorial park to see the battery. As a precaution against anyone in the city attempting to bomb the battery and hitting our camp instead, the two are sited well apart. There's also the noise factor. Although the gun isn't fired much after dark, it's still fired—with the intention of interrupting the sleep of those in the city. My guide said it makes a considerable noise, so it was placed over a rise, hidden among the trees, near an old fort from the Austro-Hungarian era.

There, soldiers manning a Browning heavy machine gun were sitting on empty ammunition boxes and smoking, waiting for orders to fire. They were unshaven, black with dirt, sloppily dressed, and, apart from when they were cursing and joking among themselves, reticent to the point of rudeness. They were riffraff (I like that word, its symmetry and pendular resonance, the switch of just one letter for another). I was reminded of Wellington's comment, along the lines of, *I don't know what effect these men will have on the enemy, but by God they frighten me.* I wouldn't have trusted them with anything, that's for sure, and my point was proven when Santo told me they frequently let off a few rounds into the city every now and again, whether or not they'd received orders to do so.

"Usually," he said, "we shell the city for a few days, then for a little time we do nothing. The enemy does not understand what is going on. It frightens them: 'Why aren't they shelling us any more, what is happening?' they ask themselves. They wonder if perhaps we have left and gone home, that's what they hope. Then we start the shelling again. It's totally random, to keep them guessing."

While we were at the battery, the Browning was fired (for my benefit, I had the feeling), the bullets ripping through the air in a deafening explosion of sound, like a stream of sperm erupting from the burning barrel of the gun. One young man—no, creature—cavorted around as if he was doing St. Vitus's dance, at times bent double, laughing and shrieking, a hand in the pocket of his baggy camouflaged trousers jerking himself off. Santo dug me in the ribs, grinning broadly, concerned that I'd missed the spectacle. The other soldiers ignored their friend, possibly having witnessed his excitement many times before, more interested in looking at Santo and me and studying our reactions. Some of them were smiling, but only with their mouths, not their eyes.

When they finished, Santo added: "The other thing they do is lob a mortar into the center of the town. It may injure a couple of people, and they cry out for help. Others rush out of their homes and shelters to care for them. A few minutes later, our boys lob another mortar onto exactly the same spot. That second one is more effective."

I made a mental note of all I was seeing and hearing as we headed back into the village. I was congratulating myself on discovering a gold mine.

Santo interrupted my thoughts. "Tell me, why are you here, Milan?"

"My father's Serbian." I thought that was the simplest explanation.

"That is a good enough reason. So you are not one of those who are just here to kill people? That is why many people come to this city: so they can shoot their fellow human beings. They think it is more fun, better sport, than shooting wild pig or wolves. They get bored shooting those."

I changed the subject. "What I don't understand, Santo, is why don't we march into Sarajevo and take it by force. Why stay up here in the hills?"

"We would lose too many of our people if we did that. The Serbs have never been good foot soldiers. We are only good with artillery. Also, the UN is down there, in Sarajevo—French, Canadian, Dutch, and your British troops, too. They would make things difficult—awkward. Anyway, the Bosnians will surrender soon, so why should we bother? But now it is my turn to ask you something, Milan: why do we allow the UN to use the airport to bring relief into the city?"

"Do they control the airport?"

"They do. They keep it so they can fly in humanitarian aid, yet they will not allow the Bosnians in the city to use the airport to escape. So they are prolonging the war: feeding the enemy, but not helping them to leave the city. That is crazy if you ask me." He slapped me on the back and laughed. He has a staccato laugh, one that fails to convey happiness—*huh, huh, huh, huh!* Having a laugh that sounds like an extended burst from a machine gun strikes me as a bonus around here.

"But there are many crazy things about this war, Milan, so why not one more?"

He then told me how the enemy had built a tunnel beneath the airport's main runway. They finished it two years ago and it's now the busiest route in the country, rumored to have as many as four thousand traveling through it every day. "At some time you will be on duty to fire at these people who sprint from the cover of the earth like badgers." I asked him where they headed after they left the tunnel. "Either into the Sarajevo suburb of Butmir, or the other way, into so-called Free Bosnia, the part of Bosnia that has not yet fallen to our troops."

We stopped for a few minutes on the way back to the camp and, like some private tour guide, Santo pointed down into the city at some of the places of interest. The Orthodox and Catholic cathedrals, a mosque, and a synagogue were all within a few hundred yards of each other, and made me think of the city's past reputation for tolerance and peaceful coexistence. He showed me the contrast between the old town to the east, with its Islamic and Oriental influences, and the wide streets and grand buildings of the newer part of the city, dating from the Austro-Hungarian occupation at the end of the nineteenth century. From the many bridges across the Miljacka River I was able to work out which was the Latin, just downstream from the National Library, where the Serbian militant and student Gavrilo Princip assassinated the heir to the Austrian throne, prompting Austria-Hungary to attack Serbia and so cause the outbreak of the First World War.

Sarajevo lay motionless and lifeless beneath its sound-stifling sheet of snow. It resembled a white tulip, the top edges of its opened petals being the mountain ridges encircling the town, its stamen, the buildings nestling at the center. It huddled in the bottom of the valley, a cowering victim on its hands and knees, its face pressed into the mud and snow, waiting for its persecutors to rain further blows on its battered body. The buildings were funneled, forced from the open plain in the west toward the rocky gorge and its rushing river, slashed into the steep mountainside to the east. On the slopes of the old town, beneath the old military fortress, the frost-covered roofs of the houses and the minarets of the mosques were piled upon each other as if in a desperate bid to escape their surroundings.

It all looked very promising.

The cold is unbearable. I've put on all the clothes I brought with me and I'm still frozen. The worst of the winter is over—or so Santo says—but I can't imagine January or February being any colder than this.

I was hugging myself by the fire earlier this evening, my frozen fingertips in my armpits, and shivering despite the flames. I basked in the heat. Sometimes I turned my back to the flames so that I'd thaw out all round. Like Napoleon's troops on the retreat from Moscow, I contemplated throwing myself onto the fire. They had done just that, and to me, now, it didn't seem like such a bad idea.

Santo ordered, "You do not go away." He walked off in the direction of the houses. Five minutes later he returned carrying an army greatcoat, the kind worn by many of the men, but at this stage of the war, so I was informed, impossible to get hold of. He put it around my shoulders.

"What's this?"

"Have you not seen a coat before?"

"But where did you get it?"

"Do not ask. It is yours now, that is all you need to know."

I thanked him, but he told me to shut up. "It is not necessary to thank me. You are my friend. Also, you are an Englishman, so you are probably a little soft." He grinned at me, pleased with his little joke.

As we ate I studied the men sitting around the fire, their faces in shadow or lit by flames. They had materialized out of nowhere as soon as darkness set in, as if from the hills, the battery, from all points on the compass. Their voices, like the flames that leapt crackling into the night sky, rose above our heads to be extinguished by the blackness.

They were genuine men of the soil. They looked as if they'd spent their lives in the fields. Their bodies and hair were caked with dirt, almost as if they'd been rolling in mud. And they were all smoking. They appeared to have been born with cigarettes in their mouths—every bit as much as they were born with rifles in their hands. From the way they held their rifles, I could see they'd been brought up with them, since childhood. They were a part of them, integral, like an extra arm. I knew fighting was a way of life for these people, that it was what they were used to, and that there had been wars in this part of the world for thousands of years, from the days when the Romans invaded in the third century BC. Peace, I think, would leave them feeling uneasy, would be a time when the world would seem out of sorts. But they've never experienced it, and that's why they're such great fighters. War is bred into them, has nurtured them, made their hands stubby fingered and their nails black and cracked. It has given them massive forearms to match. They're big men, not so much tall—although some of them are—but solid. Solid, stolid Slavs. Like great chunks of granite, they look quite immovable, ready to withstand any onslaught.

My father always claimed, "The Serbs are legendary fighters. Even though the allies have all turned on us today, they still talk about our resistance to the enemy during the Second World War. They thought we were unbeatable in battle—and so we were."

"That man over there, the one smoking a pipe," said Santo, nodding his head in the direction of a group in traditional Serb hats, standing together, laughing and talking loudly. "He has been here since 1992, when the siege started. He has not missed a day. His name is Mordo, and his brother and sister-in-law and their kids are in the city."

"They're Serbs?"

"Yes, a few of our people stayed in Sarajevo, just as many Bosnians stayed in Grbavica, on this side of the river.

Often families are no more than two or three hundred yards apart, yet they have not spoken to each other throughout the war. Many have joined us, but some still remain in the city. They are traitors, so they deserve to die. This man, Mordo, he and his relations used to shoot at each other during the day then talk over the phone at night. But now he does not know what has happened to them. They no longer speak to him, so it is possible we have shot them all."

Santo is more intelligent than the others; he told me so himself. "They are ignorant, all of them," he said after we'd eaten, indicating the men round the fire. "Peasants!" He used to be the manager of an engineering company in Sarajevo, which is why he speaks good English. He had dealings with people in Newcastle, he tells me proudly, and he reads books. "Like you, I read books, but not novels. I have no need for novels. Those peasants, however, they do not read anything. They have never read anything in their lives, not even comics."

He has a round face, almost chubby, with the inevitable drooping moustache and thick eyebrows that meet above the nose. He looks like a hairy, pugnacious baby. He reminds me of the detested Mulqueeny: the same height—or lack of—endomorphic shape, and baby face. I try not to blame him for this. Although he doesn't quite have the literary agent's tonsured look, he's definitely thinning on top. When he smiles his face lights up, but just as quickly he will stare moodily at the other men around the fire as if he despises their company.

He pointed out to me a bear of a man, well over six feet tall and as wide as two ordinary men. "That man is an animal, even more of an animal than everyone else here. His name is Bukus. Be careful of him, my friend. He is dangerous." The man appeared to be phenomenally strong. His face was deeply scarred, and his hair long and black, falling to his shoulders. His eyes were small and too close together, like a grouping on a target. The others were wary of him, I could see that. They laughed louder when he recounted his exploits, and they looked as if they would never disagree with him. He seemed quite mad, having a tendency to punch those around him at random while promising to skin others alive. I could see in his eyes that there was no one behind them, no one at home. If eyes are the windows to the soul, then his eyes had been placed in an empty house.

I recognized the man with Bukus. The two men were holding each other up, cavorting around the fire like a couple of drunks on a Soho street in the early hours. "That's Mladic, isn't it?"

Santo nodded. "He often visits the camps. Usually he's in his bunker at Han Pijesak. That's where he directs the siege from."

I was interested to see my father's hero. He looks like a square slab of pink dough, all eyebrows and hair. He's overweight, stocky, about five-and-a-half feet, with the look of a bully and a boozer. His face is sad, with a sharply down-turned mouth and deep lines running from the sides of his mouth up to the bridge of his nose, practically forming the bottom half of a cross with his eyebrows, which run at an angle of almost forty-five degrees upward from his nose. The men venerate him.

At first I couldn't place what was different about him, but finally it struck me: whereas most of the men in the camp are swathed in bandoliers, with grenades and handguns tucked into their belts and Kalashnikovs cradled in their arms, Mladic appeared to carry no weapons at all. He was wearing an army uniform but, compared to his men, he looked quite naked.

Bukus was shouting at everyone that he'd just come back from some farmhouse or other where he'd "fucked four of the whores." He was being egged on by Mladic. The giant disentangled himself from his general so he could show everyone how he'd done it to one woman. He was gesticulating like a madman, waving a bottle of wine in the air, when he reached down and, head bent forward and round-shouldered, struggled to undo his trousers. Finally he succeeded and, like a proud butcher producing a particularly fine cut of meat, took out this massive tool. I got the impression this was a regular performance and that most of the men had seen it before, yet they were still impressed. It looked like a pig's trotter hanging out of the front of his trousers. And he was waving this half-erect monster around in the air, and describing how he'd done this, that, and the other to some woman, and everyone around the campfire was laughing and cheering, some almost crying they were laughing so much, and Mladic was applauding as Bukus poured wine over his tool in an attempt, if I understood him correctly, to cool it off. Briefly, I imagined introducing this maniac to Ms. Diane, that literary agent's receptionist. He'd be sure to fuck her up good and proper. By the time he'd finished with her, she wouldn't be able to walk again for days. It would certainly stop her laughing at authors for a while.

From where I sat, watching the giant dance on the other side of the fire, lit up against the surrounding darkness, thrusting his hips this way and that in a wild parody of fornication, he looked like an incubus and a madman. But then there are enough madmen here to populate a sizeable asylum. Bukus's trousers, having by now fallen around his ankles, caused him to crash forward onto his stomach, and I swear I felt the ground shake. He rolled over and laughed, and Mladic stood over him, holding a bottle up in the air and emptying the last of its contents over the giant's face and open mouth. I don't think anyone else would have dared to do that. All the men cheered.

"You see, my friend," said Santo, "you can do whatever takes your fancy in this beautiful country of ours. Like
him"—pointing to Bukus on the ground—"you can do anything you want. For the anarchist, this is paradise. You can
murder, rape, rob, torture little children, anything you have
ever imagined, and no one will arrest you, or hold you to account, or put you on trial, or throw you into prison. There
are no police, no lawyers, no prison guards, no authorities.
You can break the highest moral law on earth and get away
with it, because it's legal. Everything is legal."

Perhaps I looked skeptical; I certainly shrugged, because he went on to tell me that it was the law of the jungle
in Bosnia now, and only the strongest would survive. He
said it was possible to do anything you wanted to another
person, and the only person who would try to stop you was
the one you wanted to kill, rape, rob, or torture. So long as
you had the strength to overcome them, then you could
do it, do whatever you dreamt of. There was nothing to
fear, nothing to worry about, ever. "And that's when a man
truly finds out the kind of person he is, whether he is good
or bad."

He pointed out a handsome, curly haired individual
nearby. "You see that man there? That is Radomir. He is
a good example of what I am telling you. He is a priest, a
Catholic priest, and he is killing people every day. He has a
rosary wrapped around his rifle, but he is shooting people
down in cold blood. He says he is doing it because he wants
our people to win back their land and then we can all live in
peace. He says he is doing God's work, but I don't believe
him. I think that is bullshit. He enjoys the killing, that is what
I think. You can see it in his eyes. He is no different from a
lot of people here. They love killing. Many of them have orgasms when they shoot someone, did you know that? And
that priest, he hears his own confession, so he is always sure

of forgiveness. They are a clever lot, those religious devils," and he shook his head at the wonder of it. He leant toward me, placing a hand on my shoulder and lowering his voice: "Once or twice, so I have been told, that priest over there has visited the farmhouse. What do you make of that?"

I didn't know what to make of it, and was too tired to ask about this farmhouse he was talking about. I was more interested in the idea that you would never be held accountable for anything you did. That was an awesome thought. That was real freedom. To know that no one will ever come knocking on your door opened up a world of possibilities. You were limited only by the limitations of your own imagination. For a novelist this place presented the opportunity to create a life, a real life, to play God.

"My friend," said Santo, his hand still on my shoulder, still trying to win my attention, "I could kill you right now and, apart from Papo—who will curse me for having wasted one of our snipers—no one will give a fuck." He laughed loudly and slapped me on the back. "Think about that."

"But then it could be me who kills you, Santo. You think about that."

He laughed even louder at what he deemed a preposterous suggestion coming from an Englishman, and slapped me on the back again.

There has to be honor among thieves, I thought, or can it be more basic than that? These animals don't kill each other and don't seem to fight among themselves, but surely only for reasons of self-preservation? It can scarcely have anything to do with conscience. They know they're safe as a group, that their common enemy is elsewhere, so they can't afford to turn on each other.

A man appeared out of the darkness, his arm extended toward me. "My name is Nikola. I am a lawyer." It was said as if it might impress me. It didn't because I'd already discovered there were lots of professionals among us: lawyers, accountants, engineers, computer people, and so on. Strangely enough it's the peasants who are in charge, the professionals in the main just being volunteers. It must be strange for them to be ordered around by those who can probably neither read nor write.

Santo whispered to me, loud enough for this Nikola to hear: "The only court this idiot has seen is a tennis court."

The newcomer's face was sad, with haunted, suspicious eyes. His hairline was receding and his shoulders sagged. He was tall and skinny, but his stomach bulged out beneath his belt like an overstuffed bumbag. He looked defeated, if not by this war, then by his own interior one.

"Why are you joining us?" Santo snarled. "Is it because Bukus won't let you near enough to lick Mladic's arse?"

Nikola ignored him, but said to me: "You must be careful who you choose to be friendly with." He then started to talk politics with me (a Serbian's main topic of conversation, as far as I can tell), sitting down and quickly launching into an explanation of the current war.

"A third of Bosnia's population is Serbian, did you know that?" He didn't wait for an answer. "And all we want, us Bosnian Serbs, is to become citizens of Greater Serbia. Is that so wrong? Already we control three-quarters of the country, so our enemies should give up now. Why do they go on fighting? It is a waste of time."

Clutching his half-empty bottle of Slivovitz, the plum brandy they all drink here, Nikola stared morosely into the tall forest of flames, the forest of trees black in the background, as if he were a student puzzling over a difficult exam question.

"These people who are so ready to condemn our actions, who do not even live here, they have no understanding of what it is like to be a Serb living under a fascist regime in Bosnia or Croatia, to be a minority. They have no right to criticize. They do not know." And he spat in the face of his critics by spitting in the dust at his feet.

"We are forced to live under a Muslim government that does not want to remain part of the Yugoslav federation . . ."

"That's not so surprising when the Yugoslav federation is Serbian dominated."

"So what?" He turned and scowled at me. He obviously didn't like to be contradicted. "It has worked well for a long time, so why change things? Why do they suddenly want to become an independent state?" He declared that when the Muslim majority voted for independence for Bosnia, and the country was recognized by both the US and the European community, the Serbs were forced into a corner. His conclusion, which scarcely surprised me, was that the war was the fault of the Bosnian Muslims. It could have been avoided; it was not what the Serbs had wanted. "We want to live among our own people, that is all."

He made it all sound so reasonable—doubtless as reasonable as the arguments of those on the opposing side. Before I knew it he had moved on to the battle of Kosovo in the fourteenth century. Doubtless he thought he was educating me. He insisted that although the Ottoman Empire conquered the Serbs, there were twice as many Turks as Serbs at the start of the battle, and twice as many Turkish dead as Serbian dead at the end. And that just about sums this place up, I thought: we were defeated, yes, but we killed twice as many of the enemy, so we really won. When I pointed out to Nikola that it was a defeat nevertheless, he snorted with rage and looked ready to kill me also. It's over five hundred years later, but he was still upset by the defeat. The Serbs, I'd already learnt, have memories like elephants.

A few minutes later he left us, looking even less happy than when he'd arrived.

"Watch him," said Santo. "He does not like you."

"You think?" I asked innocently. We both laughed.

I never spoke to the kids at school if I could help it, and they soon learnt not to speak to me. They left me alone, I left them alone, and most of the time we had nothing to do with each other. I ate my sandwich in the playground at lunchtime only if I could get the bench in the corner, beneath one of the plane trees, to myself. If I was there first, before the kids came out for their break, they didn't sit with me. It was a kind of unspoken agreement.

There was a patch of muddy grass and a large expanse of concrete in front of me. At the end of the playground there was a six-foot-high white brick wall, with a six-foot-high fence on top of that. They didn't want the kids to escape, that was for sure. Behind this wall was a laneway. It ran between the school and some playing fields, and it was where, after school hours, kids would smoke, fight, touch each other up, plan rebellions against the adult world, cover the lane-side of the wall with graffiti, and do drugs. There was no access from the playground to the laneway; the only entrance to the whole school was at the front of the building, the two sides of the grounds lined with semis keeping their respectable backs to whatever was going on among the shouting hordes of young people across the road.

I'd sit on the bench and listen to the kids—though I never made it obvious. I wanted to discover if their dreams were any different from mine when I was a kid. They were: they had bigger dreams. With every generation, the dreams get bigger, or that's the way it seems to me. During the Second World War, my mother told me, all anyone dreamt of was peace, an end to the bombing. After the war they dreamt of having work, a job, that was their dream. "In those days we didn't ask for a lot," was how she put it. But my generation, we wanted more than peace. We'd only ever known peace, and it was pretty meaningless. We wanted material things, and to be able to enjoy ourselves. Everyone I knew wanted the same stuff—the house, the flash appliances, the car—especially women, but it left me cold.

Work we never worried about. There were more jobs than there were people, and if you didn't like your job, you walked out and took another one down the road. Not like now, when you have to go on bended knee to get yourself the most menial of jobs. I started out as a teacher, went through teacher training and everything, but never took it up. One or two of us at the college dropped out, disgusted with the way the Conservatives, as with everything else, were forcing people out of the public sector and into the private one, running the system down, paying teachers less than they were worth, and allowing school facilities to rot. I became a janitor instead, because I didn't want to work in a rotten system and be paid a pittance for what I considered to be a vocation rather than a career, and because I didn't want my life's work to go totally unappreciated. Anyway, it gave me time to write. That was my dream, to be a writer.

The kids were different. Their dreams were almost too big to be contained by the walls and fences that ran around the playground. They were mega. You could interpret their dreams from the way the kids dressed. Even though many of them came from poor backgrounds, they were dressed in Nikes, Adidas, or Reeboks. They had all the gear their heroes wore. Around the basketball hoop I saw miniature Charles Barkleys, Scottie Pippens, and Shaquille O'Neals. They even imitated the stars' movements: the swagger across the court, the cool, unsmiling look, and the high fives every time they scored. It was uncanny. That's what most of them wanted to do: they didn't have time for this studying lark, they were in too much of a hurry to get across to the US of A and play for the NBA. This was true of the kids who were only four foot nothing, who'd never be allowed to even step onto an NBA court. In their dreams they not only dreamt of being the next Shaquille O'Neal, they saw themselves as being at least six foot seven. Size obviously came with the dream.

They believed all that. And if they weren't going to be basketball players, then there were two other avenues open to them. They could be either a film star or a rock star. (Girls were a little different; they dreamt of being supermodels, even the fat, spotty ones.) But they weren't dreaming all of this, that was the strange thing: to the kids this was more like reality. This is what'll happen, they told themselves, this is what I'm going to do with my life. You could see it in their eyes, the faith. Like Teresa of Avila, they had visions.

"I'm going to play for the Lakers," said one small kid, drumming the basketball on the ground.

"The Lakers suck," said his friend. "I'm playing for the Knicks or the Bulls." They sounded like it was all agreed, and they were going home later that day to pack their kit and head off to the airport.

I heard one kid say he was going to play for Manchester United, another that he wanted to be a rock star and trash hotels, another that she'd be bigger than Naomi Campbell, another that he was going to star alongside Arnie in an action movie. Sitting in the playground, I heard it all. All the kids spoke seriously, thoughtfully, as if they'd weighed up all the possible avenues of success and these were the ones they'd now chosen. They never considered failure, nor were they content to look at the possibility of being on a lower rung of the ladder, of simply being a model, joining a local band, or playing on some amateur basketball team. No, they had to be up there with Naomi, Mick, or Shaq.

I'm all for people having dreams, but these kids were dreaming way out of their league. They were fooling themselves. They were doomed to failure. They weren't going anywhere, except straight down the road to the unemployment exchange. Then they were heading back to the abusive wife and the snotty-nosed, screaming kids, the refrigerator full of beer and crap fast food, and the debt collector banging on their front door every day.

Martin Luther King had a dream, but these kids had dreams that would dwarf anything he ever had. His dreams would never have got a look in at my playground. When I was at school I had my dream too, but it was a realistic one, or so I thought—and that's what made me different from today's kids. I wanted to be a writer. Not a writer of best sellers or literary masterpieces, just a published writer. My mother was the one who did my dreaming for me most of my life, certainly early on when she had the same dreams as I did, before she got suckered in by my father.

"How's that book of yours coming along?" she asked when I visited home last summer. She's always been good like that, remembering things about people, looking as if she was taking an interest in their lives. Maybe she's genuine, I don't know. There's certainly a part of her that still hopes I'm going to make something of my life, although I suspect it's in a field other than writing.

I told her I'd finished it.

"Will someone publish it, do you think?"

"I expect so. That's the only reason I've written it."

"That's wonderful."

The way she carefully put down the dish she was holding and turned to look at me, surprise on her face, made me elaborate a little. I didn't want to disappoint. "There are one or two publishers interested." It seemed a reasonable embellishment.

"That's wonderful news, Milan." She was such a book lover, she probably had a soft spot for authors too, or that's what I told myself.

"There could be a bidding war, you know." Sometimes I can't help myself. She looked puzzled, so I elaborated. "It's like an auction. Publishers bid against each other to obtain the rights to your book."

"I always knew you'd be a success." And she picked up another dish to dry.

No, you didn't, I thought.

Of course my father couldn't stay out of it. I should have known he'd be listening. He butted in from behind his newspaper. "He hasn't done it yet. Don't count your chickens."

"But if there are several publishers interested . . ."

"Two. He said two."

"But two publishers, don't you think that's a good sign?"

I wouldn't have bothered. I'm used to him and his buckets of cold water. He's been doing that to me all my life.

"From what I've heard, they're bastards, the lot of them." My father continued to demolish my mother's dreams, her dreams for me. "Anyway, how can someone write about life when they've never experienced it? What's he ever done with his life? You tell me what he's going to write about—cleaning out the school toilets? Polishing the school corridors? Locking the school gates at night? What's he done that will interest anyone?"

"It's a good book, it deserves to be published."

"Maybe it does, but I'd have thought you'd be a sight better off with a real job. You're not going to keep a girl like Bridgette being a janitor."

He was spot on there. I was certainly right not to tell them about Bridgette and I splitting up when it happened a few months later. I often wondered why he didn't make a pass at her himself, he fancied her so much. (And, yes, I'm sure she'd be only too keen to go out with a village newsagent.)

But I believed what I'd been saying to my parents then, and I believe it now. I invested everything in that book, including three years of my life. It deserved to be published, of that there was no doubt in my mind.

"One of the publishers is even talking about film rights." I don't know why, but I always lay it on thick when I'm with my parents: they bring it out in me. I suppose it makes me feel good encouraging them—or my mother at least—to believe there's some hope.

"That's wonderful. How exciting. Would that mean you'd go to Hollywood?"

"I'd definitely like to write the screenplay. I've no desire to hand control over to someone else."

"But would you know how to do it?"

"Easy. Writing the book, that's the hard part. Anyone can write a screenplay once they've got an idea."

My mother doesn't seem to understand my desire to write, despite the fact she reads so much and loves books so much. Once she did. But now I feel as though she's betrayed the dreams we shared, like she's given up on me. All she's keen on now is for me to settle to something she perceives as a proper job—oh yes, and marry Bridgette and have a family. "Your father never held down a job for long. I blame all the upsets he's had in his life. He has a good brain, only he's never done anything with it. I wish I had half his education." Now she thinks she sees me going the same way.

Neither of them really understands what I want to do, what I want to be. I'm separate from them, outside of them, beyond their comprehension. Even though writing has always been what I wanted to do more than anything else in the world, they couldn't grasp that. It was completely alien to them.

The apartment in which I'm now writing this is in a block of six in the suburb of Grbavica. It's the same room Santo brought me to the day after I arrived in camp. "It is a good place to start," he said, as if he were dropping me off at some department in a company headquarters on my first day at work. It's also the apartment from which I failed to shoot that publisher's reader.

Grbavica was seized by the Serbs at the very beginning of the war, in May 1992. The suburb penetrates the belly of the town like the nodule on a piece from a jigsaw puzzle, stretching down from the steep lower slopes of Mount Trebevic to the south bank of the river. It's the only part of Sarajevo they've managed to capture, and it's scarcely a good advertisement for Serb rule. It's a shell, a ruin, a mass of twisted, tortured, tilted steel and concrete. The only glass is underfoot. Any surface that's still vertical is pitted with shrapnel and bullet holes. Personal belongings—crockery, books, children's toys, articles of clothing, smashed furniture—lie scattered in the streets. Garbage spills out of ripped bags, the pulped, liquefied, stinking mess licked and picked at by both skeletal dogs and humans. Great mounds of masonry block many of the roads. At night there are bursts of manic laughter, screams, shouts, gunfire, running footsteps, and smashing bottles. People flit from doorway to doorway like ghosts. Tanks rumble in the distance. I wonder briefly which is the more desirable suburb: Grbavica or across the river in the city. The six apartment blocks are down by the river. Three run east–west, and lie directly one behind the other. I'm in the front building, on the twelfth and top floor, facing the Miljacka River. The center of the city lies at about two o'clock to my position, across the reddish, tumbling waters of the narrow river. The buildings are ordinary, what I would call Eastern European trash. Behind them are many more apartment blocks, more of the same, but with fewer floors. That's their only redeeming feature: fewer floors. They're concrete rectangles, like dominoes lying on their sides, with flat roofs and row upon row of small windows. The walls are dotted with gaping holes as if someone had come along with a sledgehammer and added a few extra windows. It's a dangerous place to hang around, yet some families still skulk in the basements of the rear apartments, which are linked together by fetid, rubble-strewn, almost pitch-black corridors. These are the troglodytes of war, wrapped in rags, huddled over candles or kerosene stoves, shrinking back into the shadows whenever a sniper passes by on his way to a new aerie.

At ground level there's only dust and rubble. Doors have been removed, probably for firewood. The walls are chipped, the paint flaking, and graffiti, spidery black and uninspired, crawls at random across every surface. The rooms have been stripped bare. I sit well back from the windows on an old mattress I found downstairs. I prize it, my only possession, my only shred of domesticity. Why wasn't it removed, along with everything else? I think someone must have salvaged it for themselves, and then was forced to flee and leave it behind. Maybe they were killed in the street when they went out to get a loaf of bread or a container of water. It's more than likely.

It's important I write these notes or observations (call them what you will) as if I'm writing them for me. (But note the "you" in that sentence, sneaking in, unheralded, unwanted. Is it simply a figure of speech, or is it in fact some nameless reader I already have in the back of my mind?) I don't want to have a reader sitting in front of me, influencing what I write. They've spurned me in the past, so why should I bother with them now? When I wrote my last novel I had a reader in front of me. He was a creation, as fictional as my novel, but real nevertheless. He was my ideal audience and, when I was writing I'd ask myself, how will he take this, what will he make of that piece of news, will such and such be of interest to him? This is normal, I believe. But now I don't want him. It's too constraining to have a reader in front of you all the time. It's like a guard dog, watching your every movement with a critical eye, barking whenever he's displeased, whining when he wants something he hasn't received, attacking you should you wander off his favored path. I want to be free, to write only for myself—if that's possible. Can putting a word down on a piece of paper ever be just for oneself? I could argue that I'm keeping this journal now in order to remind myself of these incidents in my life later. But if it's not a strict reminder note—*Go to the shops and buy some butter*—then surely those words are for someone else? Ultimately.

I notice a certain reluctance on my part to pick up my rifle, my Steyr SSG. Is note taking my excuse, or is it because of the fiasco with the publisher's reader? Although I came to Sarajevo to be a sniper, I'm already wondering if I can get by with just talking to people and listening. But how long would it be before Santo and the others realized I was a fake? So I dutifully go through the motions, crouching by a window, rifle at the ready, staring across the river at the deserted city, half hoping no one will appear. But this afternoon someone did.

A man walked onto the bridge that crosses the Miljacka River just to the west of the Skenderija sports center. It's the bridge where the first person, a female student, was shot dead in the war, in 1992. The bridge has iron railings and narrow pavements on either side, with cobblestones in the center. On the far bank is a building that appears to have been skinned alive by bullets and mortars, most of the red brickwork, like raw bleeding flesh, now clearly visible. Behind it are the ruins of the Parliament.

This man strolled onto the bridge as if he had all the time in the world. Having spent a couple of days watching people run everywhere, even when they were carrying containers of water or baskets of food, such behavior struck me as unusual. It was noticeable because it was different. He was so calm and relaxed he could have been taking a stroll in Hyde Park on a Sunday afternoon. He was probably one of the suicidal ones Santo had told me about, those who stroll along the pavements of Sarajevo as if they're out shopping in London or Paris. "It is up to you if you waste those idiots. I think if they are so keen to die, we should oblige, we should help them on their way. But others say we should not help them, that we should make them suffer. Why kill them if they want to die? They say, let those who want to die, live, and let us concentrate on killing the ones who want to stay alive." And he'd slapped me several times on the back, and laughed his machine-gun laugh, and taken another swig from his bottle of Slivovitz.

I watched the man for a few minutes before raising my rifle. My hands were shaking. Seeing as he was making no attempt to keep under cover, he'd be an easy target. The nerve of the fellow surprised me. I was adjusting the SSG's sights —windage, five-to-seven east–west, distance four hundred yards—not, I have to admit, with much enthusiasm, when he reached into his jacket pocket and took out a pack of cigarettes. He lit one, as calm as anything, as if he were in a commercial extolling the virtues of this particular brand. There was a certain theatricality about his movements, as if he were acting this ever-so-cool part. It was too bizarre and, to tell the truth, I was fascinated. I could scarcely believe what I was seeing. It was so crazy, this man enjoying his last cigarette, he had me captivated. He made me smile. I decided to join in the fun.

The dust kicked up just to his left, right at his feet, but he never moved, never turned round, didn't even flinch. All he did was take another puff of his cigarette. I could see it clearly. I adjusted the rifle, took careful aim and put a shot to the other side of him, just to his right. Again I saw the dust kick up, but the man continued to puff away, leaning on the railings, staring down into the water as if these bullets cracking into the stone around him were of no concern or interest to him whatsoever. He treated the bullets like they were flies, some minor irritant, except that he was not even bothered to brush them aside. I'll say that for him, he was cool, really cool. I liked him, he didn't give a fuck about anything. I fired three or four more shots around him, the ricochets of which must have almost deafened him, but he never flinched. By this time it was as if we'd reached an agreement together; simultaneously agreeing, even though we were several hundred yards apart, that this was some kind of amusing game we were involved in, a game of bluff, a little joke between ourselves and, on my part at least, nothing fatal was about to occur. He finished his cigarette, dropped it on the pavement, ground it beneath his foot, raised his collar a little higher against the cold—as if he were the lead part in some B-grade detective movie—put his hands in his pockets, and strolled off toward the city.

And there was this argument raging in my head as I tracked the man with my rifle. I couldn't afford to let him go . . . could I? But nor was I too happy about shooting someone who was simply offering himself as a target. Why didn't he keep under cover? It was too cold-blooded to shoot him like this. By now my heart was beating so violently, I could scarcely hold the SSG steady. I had my finger on the trigger. I held my breath . . . I was struggling with indecision. And as I hesitated, the man suddenly jerked forward, his body hit with such force that he spun sideways and landed face up on the road. I was shocked. For a fraction of a second I thought I'd squeezed the trigger, then realized it must have been another sniper, possibly someone in the adjoining apartment block.

I had suspected there was one of our snipers nearby. It's scarcely surprising. There's no coordination of sniper positions as far as I can see: we don't get together every morning to be allocated places to go. It's totally haphazard, people heading off from camps around the city in any direction they want, many staying where they are overnight. But this other sniper was too close. Snipers are like large predatory animals. We need a lot of space between each other. Birds, small mammals, squirrels, and suchlike can live surprisingly close to each other, even in adjoining trees. They don't need a lot of territory. But lions, tigers, hippos, elephants—even the bears that are said to still roam these hills—they're not keen to brush up against their neighbors. They need their space, they want air. It's the same with snipers: we like a few hundred yards between us, then there's no overlapping of interests, no conflict, and we're not a menace to each other.

Work it out. The telescopic sight I'm using magnifies by the power of six. It places someone who is three hundred yards away from me just fifty yards away. Someone who is fifty yards from me might as well be in the same room. I can see the color of his eyes and the stubble on his chin. So I'm not too happy being that close to another killing machine, even if he's on the same side as me. I never forget: all that can beat a sniper is another sniper. Already I've learnt not to trust anyone.

The fact is, we had our own targets, my neighbor and I. I always divide up my area of operations as if I were slicing a cake. I'm at the center, and the thin slices fan outward as far as the eye can see. There were the bus and train stations, the National Museum, the Holiday Inn hotel, the mustard-yellow hotel where overseas journalists stay, and behind that, twin office towers. If I could shoot someone near the hotel and on Snipers' Alley—so called because it's the main road that leads out of town to the airport and is open to all of us up in the hills—there was a good chance of making it onto the evening news back home. It was even possible that my parents, sitting in front of their telly, might see one of my victims crumple to the pavement. *Look at our son. Doing a fine job, isn't he? Gone and hit another one. Makes you proud.* Some of the overseas news cameramen, I've been told, leave their videos running all day, covering the intersection in front of the Holiday Inn hotel, hoping they'll catch the actual moment someone is shot and killed. Ideally, they'd like to recreate Robert Capa's photograph of the soldier killed in the Spanish Civil War. They'd make a tidy sum for such a scoop, a well-paid, legitimate snuff movie.

My neighboring sniper must have been facing the city proper, including the old town, the main post office, the city hall and the national library, and mosques and offices. This means he'd definitely shot someone in my sector. What's more, and even more worrying, is the fact he obviously saw me shooting around the cigarette smoker, intentionally missing him. I wondered what would happen if he told everyone back in camp.

Despite the cold, I was almost blinded by sweat. The cigarette smoker lay motionless. He wasn't about to inhale again, that was for sure. I looked toward the open door, fearful that my failure, or indecision, had been witnessed. I couldn't believe I'd failed again. I told myself that I'd been close to succeeding. I'd just been unnerved by the fact the man hadn't been running, hadn't been trying to hide. I'd been frozen by his immobility, by his naked vulnerability. It would have been too close to murder. I needed him to have run, to have been like one of those rabbits in Mr. Sinclair's field darting—no, *haring*—for the safety of its burrow. Then it might have been possible.

It's his farm now. I don't know when Mr. Sinclair died, but that Andy now lives there with his mother, his wife and his young son, I do know that. When I last visited my parents, I saw him. Ran into him in the center of town, doing his Christmas shopping, immediately around the corner from where we used to go to school. He was still red haired and ruddy cheeked, just as he had been sitting next to me in class, but now he totally filled the space in front of me, a giant presence, awkward and silent. He was wearing an open-neck checked shirt—even though the weather was cold—and big boots. He looked like he did as a kid, only bigger, as if he'd been pumped up. He was still self-effacing and shy, almost embarrassed, dancing around on the pavement in front of me, grinning awkwardly. The reason we became friends at school was because he was so quiet: I could boss him around. Andy always did exactly what I told him. He wasn't simple, like Steinbeck's Lennie, just eager to please, as if his life depended on helping people. He was a little in awe of me, that's what it amounted to: despite the fact he towered over me, he looked up to me. When I saw him in the High Street all those years later, so shy I think he'd have tried to walk past unless I'd stepped in front of him and blocked his path, we reverted immediately to our old relationship.

Standing outside the same newsagent we used to visit as kids every Saturday morning with our pocket money, I could once again have grabbed the coins from his podgy hands, prized open the sausage fingers, and told him which sweets and comics we were going to buy with his money. I don't believe he'd have objected.

It was in our early teens that I became tired of him. It was boredom, I think, the fact we had so little in common. He was dull and tedious, too kind and decent. He wasn't interesting or fun to be with. And I could see now, more than twenty years later, that I'd been right: he hadn't moved on at all. His dreams—if he'd ever had any—had stopped at his property's boundary fence.

Originally, I hung around with Andy because he gave me access to rifles. I don't think he ever realized this. I'm good at fooling people when I want to. I can lead them right up the garden path while they're still under the impression they're standing at the front gate. So he never had any idea it was the rifles that kept me knocking on his farm door, none at all.

I could even claim that Andy's dad is responsible for me being here today: he taught me to shoot. I liked Mr. Sinclair; he was always laughing. "Come here, lad," he said to me one morning. "Let me show you the proper way to hold a rifle." We were standing in the courtyard outside the kitchen, and Mrs. Sinclair was watching us through the window. She was smiling. I can remember still to this day how I felt they were a real family, not like mine.

"Keep the butt tight against your shoulder. Pull it in here, that's it. But keep breathing. Breathe regularly."

He moved around in front of me. "You have to be relaxed when you're holding a rifle, Milan. Don't get tense. When you're nice and ready, as you breathe out, hold your breath, then squeeze the trigger. Don't pull it, squeeze it."

I squeezed the trigger and there was a click.

"You're a natural." He laughed, taking the rifle off me. "Did you see that, Andy? Steady as a rock. If you're not careful, he'll be as good as you one day." Andy grinned. He looked genuinely pleased.

"The rifle has to be a part of you, lad, an extension, like an extra limb. Remember that and you'll be right."

Mr. Sinclair also taught me how to clean a rifle and how to be safe and responsible—opening the rifle when carrying it. When he trusted me enough and felt I knew what I was doing, we were allowed to go out and shoot rabbits by ourselves. There were plenty of them around. We'd sneak up to the brow of this hill, overlooking a small field—the Norfolk coast and its slither of sea in the distance—and there were so many rabbits hopping around and nibbling away we could have closed our eyes and fired and we'd have likely hit one. I loved the way rabbits jump in the air when they're shot, as if they've been startled and can't hide their surprise, then crash to the ground, on their sides, absolutely still. It was like a little dance of death routine, and the contrast always surprised me: between the leap into the air and the finality with which they landed on the grass. As if miming an exclamation mark.

I remember Mr. Sinclair once asking me what I wanted to do when I grew up. He never asked Andy. His future was to be the farm, everyone knew that.

"I want to be a writer." I don't know why I told him, I'd never told anyone, not even my parents. I wanted to impress him, for him to see me as different, I think that's what it was.

"Books?" he asked.

"Yes."

"Novels?" I nodded. He looked skeptical, but said nothing more, just looked doubtful. I decided that he was neither interested nor impressed, and I was disappointed. But one evening, the very first time Andy and I went off alone to shoot rats in the two barns about half a mile from the house, he said to his son as he handed him the rifle: "And watch that friend of yours; he'll be more use with a biro than with one of these." They both laughed, and I knew they'd been talking about my dream—together, behind my back. I blushed, and wished I hadn't told Mr. Sinclair.

The moon was looming over the horizon, huge, like one of those cheap paper lamps with which students like to furnish their digs, and the air was perfectly still. The long grass was soaking, and our footsteps left a trail of dark green through a field of phosphorescence. Andy was whispering excitedly as we left the grown-ups behind us, his breath forming cartoonish thought bubbles above his head, his voice crystal clear in the crisp air. Soon he fell silent because of my lack of response. I followed his chubby legs, white and innocent in baggy shorts, across the field, detesting the complacency of his walk and the fact that he'd never, no matter how long he lived, ever wander off the path.

We were creeping through the sodden grass, quiet as mice, on the hunt for rats. Neither of us said anything as we approached the ghostly structures, perse and menacing against the trees at the end of the field. Then we were pushing open the great wooden doors, trying not to make any noise. The rats were running along the roof supports, and we caught them in the beam of our torch. One of us held the torch, the other did the shooting. The rats kept on running when they were caught in the spotlight, so they weren't easy to hit. I was good, maybe even a better shot than Andy.

That particular night, I can see it still as clear as anything. One rat was wounded, its rear legs shattered by a bullet. It fell to the ground and tried to drag itself away into a dark corner to escape. I reloaded the rifle in double-quick time and fired a second shot, at almost point-blank range, splattering the rat all over the walls of the barn as I did my best James Cagney impression: "You dirty rat, you!" Then we high fived in the gloom.

I spend a lot of time watching for people down in the city. The few to be seen scurry everywhere. They're like rats. They're caught in a trap, so I guess that's an accurate simile. They run across intersections, dart from one parked car to the next, and burrow into doorways.

Some of them even skulk behind the armored vehicles of the UN when crossing intersections. These are driven slowly from one side of an intersection to the other while small crowds of pedestrians huddle behind them, like pilot fish around a shark. How's a sniper supposed to deal with that? Not only is it unreasonable, I think it's unsporting.

I realize the people act like this because of me, even though I've hardly fired a shot. They're darting around like rats because I'm inside their heads. I'm infiltrating the minds of an entire city. It's a psychological game. I've worked that out already—a mind game pure and simple. It is like the Chinese proverb: "Kill one man, terrorize a thousand." They knew what they were talking about, those Chinese. They were saying, people don't like to gamble with a sniper. With an artillery piece they're willing to gamble, but not with a sniper. A sniper is too selective, his victims singled out, the elements of chance all but eliminated.

But this new career of mine (which I must remember to tell the school's Career Advisory Board about on my return to London) isn't exactly easy. I thought it would be much easier. Sometimes I barely glimpse a figure—looking like a hunchbacked dwarf or deformed cripple—as it springs into view from behind a building, dives into a doorway, or jumps up from beside a parked car and sprints around a corner. By the time it's registered in my brain, the person has gone, the opportunity has been missed. I haven't yet worked out the solution. Perhaps I should keep my rifle trained on one spot and hope that someone will eventually appear there, either wander across my line of fire or simply stand and wait to be transformed into a colander. It seems a haphazard way to operate, with too much left to chance and the likelihood I'll end up dying myself—from boredom.

Once or twice, just so I won't be forced to return home and tell my father I scarcely fired a shot, I let off a round into the city—often at this lamppost that stands, defiant in its loneliness, on the corner of two main roads near the National Museum. It's famous. Santo says it can be seen from many of the mountain slopes around Sarajevo, and only from the east is it completely blocked from view by a building. For this reason it's used as a target by snipers: the perfect way to adjust one's sights at the start of the day before moving on to human targets. The lamppost is chipped, marked, and scarred up its entire length, from the fancy crossbar at the top to the broad, ornate base that widens out just above the pavement. It reminds me, in its solitariness, of the lamppost in *The Lion, the Witch, and the Wardrobe*, when the children have pushed their way through the clothes in the cupboard and reached snow-covered Narnia. I almost expect to see the White Witch in the center of Sarajevo riding by on her sleigh, wrapped in furs and eating Turkish delight. I imagine shooting her, a character in a novel, fictitious, the child of C. S. Lewis, and watching the blood spread, blossoming across her white cape before dripping down onto the snow. It's obvious I can shoot people in my head, that's easy enough. No problems there.

Earlier this evening I was sitting by myself on an upturned packing chest, waiting for Santo. He'd gone to the kitchen area to collect our food. Nikola, the lawyer, wandered up. He nodded. He had a smirk on his face. "I shot a guy this afternoon."

I didn't say anything, wondering where this was going.

"He was smoking a cigarette on the Skenderija bridge. I think he wanted to be shot. He was begging for it—like a woman. It happens sometimes." He was grinning, not in a friendly way. "Some weak-kneed amateur was shooting around him. Didn't have the balls, I guess. I have no time for that. People like that shouldn't be here."

At that moment Santo returned, and the lawyer turned and walked off. I cursed the fact it had been Nikola who'd been my neighbor, the sniper in the adjoining block. He obviously knew I'd failed. I decided to tell Santo, but made it sound like I'd been playing with the victim, and the only reason I hadn't shot him—although I had intended to—was because I'd been enjoying myself too much. I didn't mention Nikola. I simply wanted to cover myself.

Santo asks me at the end of each day if I've had "any luck." I can feel the pressure building. I'm going to have to do something soon.

He—the Soho harlot, the self-proclaimed guardian of the common man's reading, the artistic sifter, the endomorphic, intoxicated literary agent—*sentenced* my words on a Monday in January, like a late Christmas present. It was my death sentence, the day my words were interred, so I remember it well. It was a great way to start the week, let alone the year.

Returned manuscripts always catch me by surprise, turning up when they're least expected. "Allow up to three months," it states clearly beneath the publisher's or literary agent's name in the *Writers' & Artists' Yearbook*. Yet in the first few weeks after sending off part of my manuscript, I will open the mailbox every morning with an air of expectation. There will be a letter today, I tell myself, because they were immediately impressed by my novel. They are so in love with the first three chapters, they want me to express post the whole of my "promising first novel" to them right away. Even better, they want me to come in and discuss my book, as well as any other ideas I might be working on, over a spot of lunch. They want me to sign a three-book deal, to know if I could do some promotional work at this year's Frankfurt Book Fair, to invite me to a cocktail party so that I can meet some of their other authors. They want to know if I could make dinner with their chairman, Lord Wordsmith. That kind of thing.

But as the weeks pass silently by, my expectations diminish and I begin to approach the mailbox with less hope. I've been disappointed before, so why should it be any different on this occasion? I'm dealing with idiots after all. I've written three novels before this one, and around eight short stories over the past ten years, and they've all been turned down, so let's not, as they say, give up the day job quite yet.

Eventually, I open the mailbox expecting nothing, or nothing except a rejection slip. And I know what to expect from a rejection slip; I know everything there is to know about rejection slips. Rejection slips are my metier.

They're usually in the form of a letter attached by a paperclip to the front page of the manuscript. A standard printed letter. I don't even have to read it. Only three words are usually handwritten: my Christian name, after the printed word "Dear," and, after a printed "Yours sincerely," the sender's Christian name and surname. In between those three handwritten words is a potpourri of clichés from the publishers' food cupboard. "Thank you for sending us your manuscript, thank you for having approached us, thank you for having given us the opportunity to view your material, thank you for letting us consider your work . . . We read your submission with interest . . . After careful consideration, we have decided it does not fit in with our list, we do not feel we would be the right publisher for your work, we see no possibility of the completed work being suitable for our list, we have to be confident of substantial sales before taking on a project . . . I fear we do not feel able to offer the representation you seek . . . I'm afraid that due to the sheer volume of material, owing to the large number of submissions we receive, as we receive around three thousand manuscripts a year . . . Regrettably, unfortunately, sadly . . ." And so on and so forth, ad nauseam, ad nauseous. "We are unable to provide you with a more detailed response, we are unable to offer individual comments, we cannot give you a more personal response, we cannot offer critical comments . . . May I take this opportunity, may I wish you luck elsewhere with another house, agent, or publisher, may I wish you every success in placing your work with another house, agent or publisher, may I, may I, may I . . ."

All of us would-be writers, all we want is something, anything that clearly shows that our books have been read by someone. Something, anything that says this letter is addressed to me alone, a letter that identifies my novel by its title and contains a few lines that will make no sense to anyone else: "We particularly like the start of chapter 2," or "Your main character develops nicely," or "The scene on the beach is powerful." Something, anything that offers just the smallest ray of hope, the tiniest bit of encouragement. Something, anything that shows the manuscript has not been flicked through cursorily, fingered tentatively like some contaminated, soiled piece of refuse picked up at the municipal dump. Something, anything that demonstrates the publisher appreciates the effort that's gone into the book, the blood, sweat, and tears, the early morning tossings and turnings, the late-night agonies. Something, anything . . . just something more than nothing.

If publishers and literary agents are only ever going to send out standard rejection slips, why wait three months to do so? Why don't they return books within the week? Why go through the pretence? Why don't they simply take the manuscripts out of their envelopes; transfer them straight to the stamped, self-addressed envelopes that have also been enclosed; chuck in the rejection slips; and toss the lot into the Out basket? (Ms. Diane at Mulqueeny & Holland could teach them how to do this, I'm sure. *An Introduction to Rejections, Part One.*) These publishers and literary agents are going to reject the books anyway, no matter how good they are, so why bother to pretend they've read them? Why even invite people to submit their manuscripts in the first place? They aren't interested, so why pretend they are? I know why, of course. It's because publishers are small-minded, contemptible people, slaves to fashion, and only interested in how much money's in it for them.

Only once, for my last book but one, did I receive a personal comment. It pleased me because it showed that someone cared enough to take the trouble to say what they thought, but made me angry for weeks after because it had been so negative. I can still remember the exact words: "The content is literary but the writing is not." That was all they wrote.

After a few more weeks of nothing, of no news and no rejection slip, there comes a time when, perversely, my hopes are rekindled and I begin to think that my latest book won't be rejected after all. The longer they keep my manuscript, the more my hopes rise. I see positive signs everywhere. I start to believe I'm about to be discovered. I'm like some country or continent in the Middle Ages, as yet unexplored, but someone is about to set foot on me, put me on the map, acknowledge my existence, claim me as their own.

This particular morning, this terminal Monday, I remember well. It must have been a premonition because I phoned the school and said I was sick. I couldn't stand the idea of their inanities that day, the mud in the corridors, the blocked toilets, the rundown equipment, the musty smell of chalk and the rancid smell of sweating kids, the running feet and raised voices, the sheer childishness of the place. And Gilhooley knocking on the door of my small cupboard beneath the stairs and demanding in his cold, high-pitched voice why there is not a clean towel in the masters' washroom, why I haven't yet fixed the light bulb in 6C, or why have I not yet painted over the graffiti in the playground. Gilhooley, with his education theories changing faster than the departure board at Heathrow, his timetables, rosters, and budgets, his team of middle-aged, brain-drained incompetents who couldn't have rustled up a vocation between them if their lives had depended on it.

I stayed in my flat all morning. I enjoyed the secrecy of being by myself and no one (apart from the foul-breathed, spinsterish school secretary) knowing where I was. Even Bridgette, now that we'd split, didn't know where I was. I lay in bed until late, reading. I had the window closed, but the gas fire wasn't working, so the small room was still cold. Outside, I could hear the rest of the world either at work or on the way to work, and it made me feel good. The pest control man who lives upstairs with his ratlike wife and un-ratlike litter of two, was shouting as he slammed his front door and stomped down the stairs. I heard him start his van and drive off, his engine soon drowned in the steady roar of traffic on Shoot Up Hill. Eventually I got up, cooked myself a fried breakfast, then lay on the sofa and listened to Mozart's *Requiem*. I pondered the subject of my next novel. I was determined to keep writing, to get my follow-up novel, my next published novel—the all-important, notoriously difficult second novel—on to the production line. I had to be ready to go as soon as my first novel was accepted. I was determined not to be one of those one-novel wonders. This, after all, was to be my life from now on. I was to be a successful novelist, my dream was about to become reality, I was that confident.

When I went downstairs in the early afternoon I ran into Mrs. Dawes. She and her husband live in one of the ground-floor flats. I rarely saw him, and I only saw her on those occasions when, muttering to herself, she limped around the front and sides of the building, picking up the empty beer and whisky bottles that materialized there most nights, or if she managed to intercept me in the company of "darling Bridgette" (her words, not mine), whom she doted on, like the daughter she'd never had and all that garbage. The senile creature was telling me something about her husband—who never ventured farther than their front door—and how he hadn't been the same, not since that terrible thing happened to Sharon Stone. That was their cat, named after the American actress. I always wondered if the cat used to sit on the sofa, crossing and uncrossing her legs—fleetingly revealing her pussy—being interrogated by Mr. and Mrs. Dawes. I never got round to asking her, however, and now it was too late to ask her anything.

To tell the truth, I'd been glad to see the beast's back, rigor mortis straight, because I'd had a gutful of both Bridgette and that animal by then. "Oh you're so beautiful," she used to say when she came round to stay with me, bending down, stroking the cat's head and tickling her ears. "You're the most beautiful cat in the world. Are you coming upstairs with Mummy for your little treat then?" Never having heard of a woman giving birth to a cat before, not even in the *Sunday Sport*, I took it upon myself to congratulate her as we climbed the stairs. She must obviously be something of a medical phenomenon.

"Don't be like that, Milan. You know what I mean. It's my way of being affectionate." Then, addressing the puckered buttonhole disappearing up the stairs ahead of us: "You're so cute, so beautiful." Sometimes I think she even used the word "diddums"—and I'm sure that word is not to be found in any reputable dictionary.

The fact is, I should have told Mrs. Dawes that Bridgette and I had split up, then she might not have bothered me any more. As likely as not she'd have left me alone. But for some reason I could never bring myself to make the effort to do this. I think she'd have taken it as an admission of failure—on my part of course—and then she'd have had a field day blaming me, either with "I could tell he wasn't good enough for the likes of her," or with silence and reproachful stares.

But right then she was still talking, something about the pest control man giving her the creeps and how could a man do such a thing all day, living with rats ("It's not natural, if you ask me"), when I turned away and opened my mailbox. And there it was. I knew immediately. It's not every day I receive a bulky A4 manila envelope addressed to myself in my own handwriting. It lay at the bottom of my mailbox, like a dog turd on the sitting room carpet. I stared at it, and it stared back at me, trying to look innocent, but with a definite air of belligerence about it. "So! So, it's me. Yes, I'm back again. Tough. Get a move on. Lift me out of here, will you?"

I brushed past Mrs. Dawes and strode away, ignoring the loud tut of disapproval aimed at my back. I turned off the main road and walked along several narrow suburban streets, past semidetached houses with bay windows and white lintels and neat front gardens, an abandoned tricycle or football lying on the occasional front path. I was heading for the local park. I wanted to be alone. Even though I was wearing only jeans, a T-shirt, and a denim jacket, I was unaware of the cold.

The park was empty except for a lone jogger running repeatedly up and down the steep path that led to the café and the children's playground. It struck me as a particularly Sisyphean exercise. For a few minutes I couldn't bring myself to open the package. It lay on the bench next to me. We were like an old couple enjoying the peace of the park. The difference was that I felt powerless: my fate had been decided by someone out there, a literary agent whose reality, to me, consisted of no more than a few lines in the *Writers' & Artists' Yearbook*. This literary agent was about to tell me how to live my life, direct my future, and there was nothing I could do about it. Abruptly, unable to stand the tension any longer and wanting the suspense to be over and done with, I picked it up. I opened the envelope and pulled out my manuscript. Attached with a paperclip to the front page was the usual rejection letter, but at the bottom was a scrawled, almost indecipherable comment: "Scarcely original. Feel I've read this before." For a few minutes I was stunned, my brain anesthetized by shock. After three years of work, after all that sweat and effort, after the agonies of struggling with thousands of sentences, painfully pondering paragraphs, honing and polishing countless phrases, after agonizing over every word and syllable, I had received a seven word dismissal—along, of course, with the standard five or six lines of utter and total impersonality.

Yet I'd have been satisfied with so little, with the most modest of morsels. "Your novel shows promise" would have made me happy. "We would be interested to see anything else you might write" would have made me ecstatic. Just more than this insulting, anonymous dismissal.

I looked down at the rejected manuscript. It was in pristine condition. I didn't get the feeling it had been handled by anyone other than a kid-gloved postman. I can't believe I'd actually said to Bridgette, "I'm optimistic about the people who have it now. I have a feeling about them, a good feeling." I'd been talking about the Mulqueeny & Holland literary agency. I hadn't yet heard from them, and I'd begun to feel positive. I knew my argument lacked depth, that it was scarcely persuasive, I was aware of that. I also realized Bridgette could turn out to be right—as she'd so blithely pointed out to me—that my novel was destined to go the same way as its predecessors. At times she could be so encouraging.

"I think you need to face up to reality, Milan. You know how hard it is to get published nowadays, you've told me so yourself. I don't mind if you keep trying, if that's what you want, but I think you should get a proper job as well."

It's true my writing career path to date has followed a perfectly straight, perfectly horizontal line that has resisted every temptation to deviate toward the vertical. It's flatter than a dead man's electroencephalogram. The struggles I've had, the self-sacrifices I've made, the agonies I've endured, have been for what? Where's my reward? I've written thousands of words, hundreds of thousands of words, that only I have ever read. An audience of one is all I've ever managed to rustle up, an audience of one—and that's me. There has been no crowd of admirers, no gathering, no group, not even a couple. We are talking here about the onanistic ravings of the self-deluded, the scream in the middle of the night ignored by all and sundry. We are talking about my story, my interpretation of life, the information I wish to impart—*my* information—not raising the slightest flicker of interest from anyone. It makes me sick. I am hollow, empty inside, and yet I want to vomit. Killing Mulqueeny, I thought as I sat in the park, would definitely give me some relief.

Instead of going back to the Grbavica apartment, I decided to try somewhere new. I want to get away from Nikola. Also, staying in one place for too long makes it too easy for the enemy to pinpoint your position.

Mladic has declared that we're allowed to enter any house or apartment in the suburb at will. The owners are forbidden to lock their doors. And our soldiers can also help themselves to any food and drink, articles of clothing, or family heirlooms they happen to find. If they want to set up a sniping post in the front room they can do that too, despite the fact it will place the family in considerable danger. Being a bit of a believer in "an Englishman's castle" and that kind of thing, I prefer to search out an empty apartment for myself. There are plenty of them around.

My new apartment (that has a certain ring to it) isn't far from the camp, which is south of here, about a thousand feet higher up and on the other side of the Pale road. I weigh up spending the night alone or sitting beside a fire with the others. Already I'm tired of their inanities, their shallow posturing and thoughtless patriotism. Sometimes it's preferable to be alone. So long as I bring sufficient food with me, I'm quite comfortable (I have a good sleeping bag). No one seems to be interested in, nor care where, I spend the night, which makes me wonder, should I be killed, how long it will take before someone realizes I'm missing. I eat tinned food, mainly—available from the canteen. It's not unpleasant. There's a stove in the kitchen, but of course the gas has long since been disconnected or, more likely, the supply station has been bombed out of existence. The same is true of the water, which I have to collect from outside every morning. When I first arrived here, I could fill my container with snow from the drifts still piled against the walls of the apartment blocks and melt it over a kerosene camp stove. Now the snow in Grbavica has all but disappeared.

The surrounding streets remind me of home. The apartments are dilapidated and rundown, like council flats, the only difference being that London buildings aren't usually riddled with bullet holes. I imagine I can hear the conversations of the previous inhabitants on the stairs, the shouting of the kids, the slamming of doors, the raised voices, and the laughter. Where are they now, these ghosts? Where did they flee to? If still alive, they could be imagining me moving between the walls they'd once called their own. I half expect them to walk through the front door and say, "Excuse me, this is our apartment, would you mind leaving, please?" Then I'd be forced to shoot them. I wouldn't be keen to move, that's for sure.

Already I'm becoming used to the continual bombardment, the sounds of traffic and factories in any normal city replaced here by gunfire. It never stops throughout the daylight hours. Cannons boom in the surrounding hills, and when the shells explode in the streets below, everything shakes, even the ground on my side of the river. This shaking must do more damage to people's heads than the shells themselves. It must wear them down. There's also the hammering of machine guns and the whistle of artillery shells flying overhead, both punctuated by the flat crack of rifle fire from the snipers ringing the city. I always hear the report first. It can be from the mountains behind me, or in front, or to one of the sides. The city is surrounded by mountains—it nestles.

We all watch and wait, those in and around the city, each wondering if a particular missile has our name on it. That's an interesting expression: this missile *has your name on it.* John Smith, Flat 3, 54 Elm Walk. Who decides which name goes on the missile, then addresses it, writing the name and address neatly on the cone before posting it? God, is He the addressor? The waiting doesn't take long in reality, before a building in the city erupts in smoke and dust, exploding with varying degrees of impressiveness, flames sometimes shooting skyward moments later.

After advice from Santo, I now have a balaclava, a black one, which I stuff daily with an article of clothing, affix a pair of dark glasses to, and then, with a small forked stick I keep specially for the purpose, slowly raise a few inches above the window ledge. I call this "head" after the headmaster who made my job as a school janitor so miserable. My feelings toward Mr. Gilhooley are ambivalent. While wishing someone would put a bullet through his cotton-filled brain because of the way his namesake treated me, I also appreciate the fine job he's doing on my behalf. Because of this, I hope and pray he'll not be spotted.

"Come on, Gilhooley," I say as I expose him slowly to the enemy, "let me know what you can see out there." It has to be admitted that he volunteers for this dangerous work without hesitation, and I have nothing but admiration for the way in which he conducts himself. He is both selfless and patriotic, never once complaining or requesting a change of duties. So far he's been fortunate: no one has taken a shot at him. When I eventually lower him back onto the floor, uninjured, and take his place, I can almost hear him give a sigh of relief. Mission accomplished, without mishap.

My days are dominated by two activities: trying to keep warm and trying to shoot people. I wish shooting people was a more strenuous activity. I'm perpetually numb with cold, my hands and face blue. Lying prone on the ground, scarcely moving for most of the day, doesn't help. Although I wear so much clothing I can't imagine a bullet ever penetrating so many layers, some part of my body will still go into cramp on a fairly regular basis. I try to flex my muscles while remaining still. I make minute adjustments to the rear sight to allow for elevation and to the side sight to allow for windage, persuading myself that such tiny movements help to move blood through my veins, even though it's already acquired the consistency of thick syrup. I pray for a target to appear, and it does, every so often. But it's a challenge. We're talking about someone who's usually several hundred yards away, visible only for seconds, and, to make it even harder, doubled up and running. It's similar to a funfair shooting gallery: the target pops up and drops back down, or flashes across your line of vision. You don't get much time. You have to be quick, instinctive. And that's what saves me.

I didn't have time to think about shooting my first victim, my first *real* victim. It was a man. He was running across an intersection. I fired. He fell. He didn't move. I didn't either. I remained staring through the sites, stunned. I'd killed someone, and I'd done it without a moment's thought. It could have been a training exercise. I just had time to spin around and spew onto the bare floorboards behind me.

When I turned back, the man lay crumpled on the pavement, face down, one arm reaching out above his head, the other squashed beneath his body, his legs neatly together and quite straight. Electrical activity in his brain must have fizzed and crackled to a halt. His blood was creeping, slow as lava, toward the edge of the pavement. He was dead. I was numb. Time passed.

No one was to be seen. This was scarcely surprising. I've heard sniper victims are often left for hours where they fall, until someone decides an incident happened sufficiently long ago for it to be safe to venture out into the street to retrieve the body. If someone is obviously dead, it does seem pointless risking a sniper's bullet in order to go out and claim a corpse. This is understandable behavior. Human nature being what it is, this isn't surprising. I wish it were. I'd like to see someone behave in a manner that did surprise me, that made me say, "Now, I've never seen anyone behave like that before." But I can't see it happening. The predictability of human beings is all too predictable.

I lay on my stomach looking down on the scene, again aware of the cold and the taste of vomit in my mouth. I forced myself to lie still. I expected something to happen, but nothing did. I peered through the telescopic sights at a concentrated area, then lowered the Steyr an inch or so and took in the broader view. All remained quiet. Eventually I edged back from my vantage point. When I was out of sight I rolled over and sat up. I was stiff with cold. I couldn't stop shivering. I lit a cigarette, leant against the wall at the back of the room, hugging my knees to my chest, my rifle propped at my side.

And that's how it happened. That was number one. I was no longer a virgin.

I told Santo that night back at camp. I'm ashamed to say I felt a little boastful—proud of what I'd achieved, yet guilty at the same time. He insisted on toasting my first kill with several glasses of Slivovitz and shouting at anyone who'd listen that the Englishman had shot his first Muslim. My back was slapped by many people, including some I'd never seen before. I saw Nikola sitting a few yards away. He didn't congratulate me, just sat and smirked as if he didn't believe a word of it. I ignored him. I watched Santo instead. He'd wrested my rifle off me, placed it across his knees, and, with the blade of his knife, was busy scratching a small line, the first one, about half an inch long at the end of the butt. "I do it near the base," he said, "because you must leave room for all the others."

Now that I have number one carved into my rifle—a whitish scar against the green stain of the plastic butt—and supposedly the person who'll always have a special place in my heart, I have become like all the others. I am reassured. Now we are brothers.

Most days there are wounded in the camp. They're passing through, being moved to Pale or, in the more serious cases, to Belgrade. I feel I'm not the only one who doesn't like having them around. Being forced to listen to their moaning, their groans of pain, and the way they sometimes scream makes me feel uncomfortable. I prefer the wounded to remain at the far end of my telescopic site, several hundred yards away. Here, they often lie on their camp beds, motionless, as if they're already dead. One of them was being carried past me on a stretcher the other evening and he suddenly reached out and grabbed my arm. I tried halfheartedly to shake him off, but he clung all the tighter. It was in the middle of a downpour. A bloody bandage was wrapped around the top of his head, and the rain was causing rivulets of blood to run down his face. His eyebrows were arched, his eyes staring, and he said something I didn't catch, or couldn't understand. It sounded like a question. He hung onto me, waiting for an answer. The rain was drumming on the canvas that had been thrown across his body, and I stood in the mud, cursing under my breath, wanting to escape. I looked at one of the orderlies carrying the wounded man for help, but he only shrugged. He didn't seem to understand either. I didn't know the answer the wounded man was looking for, so I tore my arm from his grip, almost yanking him off the stretcher and onto the ground, and the stretcher bearers carried him away through the curtain of water. It made me feel sick.

Among those who haven't been wounded, there's a definite camaraderie. I think this is because we're all beyond the Pale, outside the bounds of civilized society. Having the rest of the world against us brings us closer together. It's certainly something I've always found appealing: having everyone hate us has never bothered me. The truth is, I like that. It makes me more determined than ever to thumb my nose at them. Yes, I like having the whole world against us, and having the opportunity to play the part of the bad guy. None of us cares what they think. Again and again I hear men saying, "They can fuck off!" "Fuck them!" "To hell with that lot!" Sometimes they're talking about the people of Sarajevo, but most of the time they're talking about the UN, the representatives of those on the inside. Although the men were suspicious of me at first, they now believe I've betrayed their enemy, which amounts to virtually everyone else in the world. I've changed sides, or that's how they see it. In their eyes I'm a fellow collaborator.

Often the talk that is carried on in the camp is between two people. It's whispered, like a confession, often earnestly, and can't be heard by anyone else. There's also a lot of grunting. Many of the men will grunt rather than speak. They'll grunt when they take their plates of food off the cook, grunt at the person sitting next to a vacant spot by the fire to find out if it's free, grunt instead of answering yes or no to someone's question.

Is that what they've become, animals living in the forest, grunting, eating, sleeping, fornicating, lying down in the mud, warming themselves by the fire, barely communicating with each other, concentrating solely on the basics, cut off from the world, doing what they're doing for no reason other than that they've been told to do it? By Milosevic, I suppose.

Sometimes there's singing around the campfire. It can be just one man with a guitar, or it can be everyone present. In the main they're folk songs, some of which I recognize from childhood. When everyone sings, an air of maudlin sincerity descends, the men either closing their eyes, lowering them to the ground as if overcome by emotion, or raising them to the pitch-black sky as if seeking an answer to their struggles here on earth. Occasionally they'll dance the kolo, a local dance. I don't join in. They dance in the mud because there's no grass in the campsite. They dance, not in celebration, but in order to give themselves comfort.

The campsite is the focus point for the surrounding area. Old friends greet each other, soldiers who haven't met for awhile clasp hands or shoulders and shout affectionate obscenities at each other, standing eyeball to eyeball. Others sit in silence by the fire, brooding, clasping their bottles of Slivovitz, being consumed by the alcohol and the flames. The crackle and whine of patriotic music on Radio Belgrade fades in and out in the background. A few of the men hunch over the transistor like relatives around a deathbed, hoping to catch some final words of wisdom, an explanation for what's happening in their lives. Some information.

If I am to fathom my presence here, then I must make sense of my past, no matter how improbable it might seem. If I cover enough pages of this journal, will everything become clear? If I write about my parents, Bridgette, my childhood, my life as a janitor, and my writing, if I put it all down on paper, black scribbles on a white page, will a pattern begin to emerge? That's one of the reasons I'm writing this—but not the main one—to explain to myself how I got here, and why. Is there a pattern in my life, in anyone's life, or is it all meaningless and point-less? I stumble through this existence and all the peaks and troughs of my past, so prominent and intense at the time they were experienced, become flattened with the passing of each year. Everything assumes the grey mantle of un-importance, and the person living this life now, me—in the fleeting present—wanders in a daze of incomprehension through it all, struggling to find my bearings.

Martin Amis writes about this conundrum, this ques-tion without answer. He says there is no structure to life, there are no patterns, and that's precisely why he writes: to create a structure, an understandable reality. Or that's how I interpret what he writes. If he's correct, then by writing a journal maybe one can step back far enough to see a pat-tern, to discern a thread weaving through all those experi-ences. But creating a link that connects everything feels too rational to me. It's been thought up by someone sitting in front of a computer.

Why am I doing this? My need to escape the stifling conformity and boredom of London doesn't explain any-thing. Possibly there is no reason, no motivation. There are many authors—and Martin Amis is just one of them—who don't believe in motivation, who think there is no A plus B equals C to life. They say a person will lie for absolutely no reason. Their characters don't act because of something that happened in their past; their actions are random. This, those authors claim, reflects life. So they feel they're perfectly within their rights to impose order on chaos. Someone has to. Quite bluntly and without shame, they manipulate. They don't even try to hide this from their readers, in fact they do everything possible to make sure their readers never forget it, and make it a feature of their novels. They're more than happy if the reader sees them pulling the strings in the background, like the puppeteer at some Norfolk beach, behind the curtain in the Punch and Judy tent, making little attempt to hide himself from the kids.

In *The Information*, Martin Amis drops in and out of the story, making little comments here, there, and everywhere like some one-man-band Chorus from a Greek tragedy supplementing the performance of the actors on stage and telling the reader what he thinks about the various characters and events. I imagine him writing a novel about the chaos of this war, of the siege of Sarajevo. He wouldn't be able to help himself. He'd be in there, pushing his Mladics and Karadzics around like a chess grandmaster, even manipulating the UN and NATO, pretending he had some control over these events that no one else has any control over.

Who is more delusional, I wonder, the Author or the General, neither of whom—and this is the reality—has the ability to understand, let alone encapsulate, what's going on in his world. It's no different to the ant I can see in front of me now, struggling across the debris on the forest floor. To make a point, I reach forward and squash it beneath my thumb. Did it understand what was happening to it, did it have any control over that critical moment? I think not. But then it's possible, I guess, that he may only have been an army ant.

So maybe I should start with Bridgette, try to make sense of her, too—although, with hindsight, I don't feel she's provided me with quite as much novelistic material as I might have hoped for at the beginning of our relationship. Something of a disappointment in that respect, I'd say.

Although I'm a little hesitant to compare myself to the dashing Vronsky in *Anna Karenina*—to hell, why not!—who rushed off to this part of the world in order to help the Serbs free themselves from Turkish rule and to forget the pain he felt over Anna's death, the similarities are startling: I'm here to help the Serbs free themselves from Bosnian rule and to forget the pain I feel over Bridgette's death—yes, yes, yes! I don't wish to be too melodramatic about this but, for me, Bridgette has died. She's rigor mortis dead, like Sharon Stone the cat. She may as well have thrown herself under a train, too, like Anna. There again, perhaps it's Sergei Koznyshev, Lenin's half brother, I should compare myself to. He accompanied Vronsky, having just spent six years writing a book on government and having it published to virtually no acclaim and only one—negative—review. What's more than obvious is that both men volunteered to further their own ambitions rather than to altruistically help the Slavs. And that reminds me of a certain someone too.

The first thing that comes to mind is that she doesn't appreciate that I'm doing something different with my life by coming here. She can't even understand why people want to travel—"What do you want to go and see other countries for; what's wrong with where you are?" If I read her this journal she'd say, "That's nice, Milan." That's one of her favorite words—which just happens to be my least favorite word. Nice. I loathe its prissy, spinsterish meaninglessness. I'd say it was the antonym of fuck or something. "You have a nice way with words, Milan," she always said. "I wish I could write half as well as you." And I'd mentally retch.

I called her to say I was going to Sarajevo. Even though we weren't together any longer, I think, in a moment of weakness, I'd hoped for tears. You know, celluloid emotions. Weeping mothers and wives on the steam-covered railway platform as their men leave for the front. Granite statues of women in an autumnal cemetery, heads bowed beneath their hoods and falling leaves, hands clasped against heaving bosoms, awash with rain and tears, that kind of thing. But no, not our Bridgette. She seemed downright indifferent, displaying an authorial distancing I'd have been proud of. She was more intent on telling me she'd gone out with one of the so-called creatives in her advertising agency a couple of times. Already! Had I been forgotten so quickly, cast aside with such speed? "I like him. He's nice." That word again. But it made me think, much against my will, of her already spreading her legs for someone else. It also made me reminisce—which is rarely advisable in situations like these.

This is how it started, the beginning of the end—which came more than three years after the beginning.

"You'll never be a writer because you can't empathize with people. You're too caught up in your own feelings to understand how someone else feels." That's what she said to me the last time I saw her, before she left my flat forever. After three years of pretending to believe in me and pretending to support my endeavors, she suddenly did a complete backflip and revealed her true feelings. She turned. Turned is right. Like a leaf in autumn, like a sunbaker on the beach, like a Rottweiler, like a worm, she turned. Like all women, she turned.

I couldn't believe it, couldn't believe she'd been lying to me all this time. She'd only been pretending to believe in me as a writer, and now she was saying she didn't have faith in me at all. All those words of encouragement were just bullshit, and when she said, "Don't give up, Milan, you'll make it, they'll recognize your talent one day," she obviously hadn't meant it at all. It had been lies from beginning to end, totally insincere. Women are so devious, despicable, and two-faced, it's staggering. Although I can't get my head around such duplicity, I think I have a sneaking admiration for such a persuasive and professional performance.

For a while she had inspired me—for a while. She was emotional, not in the sense of shouting and crying, but in the sense that she lived through her heart rather than her head. That's what appealed. She was a woman who became emotional at the slightest excuse. I found this attractive, for a while. It made her seem alive, and more involved in life than me. I felt she could open new worlds to me, feminine worlds, new experiences. When we saw a puppy in the street, she had to go up and stroke it. *What warmth*, I marveled. When we sat in a field, she made daisy chains. *How natural*, I told myself. When we sat in a café and watched passers by, she stared in wonder as if she'd never seen people before. *So sensitive*, I felt. When we went to the cinema together, invariably she'd say, sobbing in her seat, blowing flabbily and damply into her handkerchief as the credits rolled and the lights undimmed, "That was so beautiful." Although I thought this was dim, certainly none too bright, I was fascinated at the same time. There wasn't an ounce of cynicism in her—despite working in the advertising business. It was both uncanny and unnerving.

She definitely changed over time. Since we first started going out together, she'd become more her own woman, more argumentative—"standing up for myself, my rights" is how she'd probably have put it. She started to see her work—in the fake world of advertising, for heaven's sake!—as being as important as my writing. She couldn't see the difference. She became ambitious for herself, and got increasingly caught up with her quick-witted, smooth-talking, Hugo Boss'd colleagues, especially the *creatives*, the glib salesmen of washing powders, baked beans, and hemorrhoid creams; coveters of international awards; pursuers of the latest hot young directors; and frequenters of five-star restaurants. "Honestly, Milan," she'd gush, wide-eyed with that same admiration she'd once bestowed on me, "some of the scripts they write are just so brilliant; really clever and off the wall. I don't know how they come up with such ideas, I could never do it." Her attention span, which had never been awe inspiring, shrank to thirty seconds.

I argued with her about the immorality of being involved in an industry that fed the discontent of the proverbial man in the street, the common man—neatly labeled, boxed, and categorized in the C socioeconomic group; how her genius *creatives* filled this unfortunate individual with unrealizable dreams, flogging utopias of materialism that he could never—never ever—hope to attain.

I tried to explain to her, in simple words of one syllable, the error of her ways. "Why dangle carrots, like the excessive luxury and breathtaking speed of a top-of-the-range BMW, when the average fellow is going to have to make do—if he's fortunate—with a clapped-out, rattling, ten-year-old rust bucket? With vinyl seating," I added for good measure.

"But it gives them something to strive for, Milan. It gives them hope. Why shouldn't these people have their dreams, too? Why shouldn't they have their ambitions? You have your dreams, why shouldn't they?"

"Because their dreams are unattainable, that's why. They'd have to win the lottery to buy a BMW, you know that. And the same goes for the Poggenpohl kitchen, the holiday in the Bahamas, the Rolex wristwatch, and the Mont Blanc pen. They're not even likely to be able to afford a pair of Calvin Klein jeans, for fuck's sake."

"You exaggerate, Milan. You always do, you go completely over the top. You can't discuss anything normally, calmly, like other people. You just go crazy. And it's simply not true what you're saying. People want a better life, and they want to believe they can achieve it. That's what they hope for. And that's what we give them: hope. I don't think there's any harm at all in encouraging people to better themselves."

Such arguments became more and more regular. Little Miss Wide Eyes started to stand up for herself in a most unhealthy way. I found it most disconcerting. She no longer took things lying down, well, apart from *that*, and even *that* became much less frequent. One evening in early December (I can see now that she'd obviously been keen to clear the decks for the first of the advertising industry's excessive Christmas parties), after we'd eaten and quite without warning, she came out with those dreaded words: "We need to talk." No other four words in the English language can strike such dread into the heart of man. I grunted, struggling for a mix of noncommitment and disinterest. It was so unlike her to speak out, to have her say, but I knew with absolute certainty that she was about to make her bid for independence. All I had to do was decide on my reaction to this.

She said something about admiring me for being so single-minded about wanting to be a writer, and about putting everything else aside to concentrate on that. I could hear the "but" coming, galloping like the cavalry over the horizon to rescue her, and sure enough . . .

"But I want more than this, Milan."

At that moment I remember being more stunned than angry. I couldn't believe what I was hearing; I'd just cooked her dinner—a very tasty spaghetti bolognese. And how was it possible I'd allowed her to get in there first, to put the boot in before me—which I was thinking about doing anyway?

She went on to suggest that she'd given me a year to crack it as a novelist, although I have no recollection of this, and that after a year (which I gather was now up), I either had to have succeeded or I had to get a proper job—by which I suppose she meant being a copywriter on a toilet paper account and writing about the "nice, puppy-dog softness." That was her idea of writing.

She went on to point out, very considerately, that I hadn't become, during the past year, a best-selling author, nor had I even managed to become a published one. "I'm not happy going out with a janitor, Milan—a janitor who's thirty-six, as well. I'm ashamed to tell people what you do. I'm sorry, but it's true. It's embarrassing."

"You forget I'm a qualified teacher. The only reason I'm a janitor—apart from it giving me the time to write—is because the education system in this country stinks, thanks to your Conservative friends." She'd once confessed to me, to my absolute disgust, that she voted Conservative. She admired Thatcher's "strength and purpose," was the cliché she used, and now Major was carrying on the Iron Lady's good work. "You can tell your friends I'm a teacher if it makes you feel any better."

"Often I do," she said, quite without shame. "What I'm saying is"—she was trying to get back on track—"I don't know where this relationship of ours is going, but I do know it's not working."

"Count yourself lucky I'm a janitor," I said, trying again to get us off the track she wanted to be on. "If I were a genuine writer, I'd be on the dole. I wouldn't waste my time even being a janitor."

"You're not listening to me, Milan. I'm being serious."

This wasn't about my job, or not entirely, I could see that. It was summed up in that sneaky second sentence: "I don't know where this is going." I knew with absolute certainty that the "commitment" word was hovering above our heads somewhere, waiting for an opportunity to insinuate itself into the conversation. She wanted to get married. She wanted to settle down. She probably wanted babies. And sure enough, she added, "I'll be twenty-five next year, and I want more than this, before it's too late."

I looked at her. I frowned. I pretended not to understand what she was talking about. It wasn't difficult.

"Our relationship . . ." she started, but stopped. She changed tack. "You're not happy, Milan, and I'm not happy. That's about it right now. It's that simple."

"Don't put words into my mouth."

"All right then: I'm not happy."

Which is when I made the mistake of asking, "And why's that? Why aren't you happy?"

It all came out, pouring out, in a flood. How selfish I was, how I used her, how I was never there for her, and that the only thing that interested me was my writing. "You don't have time for a relationship, Milan, that's as clear as day to me. You're totally caught up with your writing."

I denied it all, of course; I felt obliged to. I didn't like this new person, this creation of mine, like a rather pretty Frankenstein stepping down from the operating table and telling me, its creator, what was wrong with me. The script was wrong; it certainly wasn't anything I'd penned.

"I've tried so hard to make it work, but it has never been enough for you." She had her handkerchief out now and was twisting it into horrible shapes in her hands, obviously wanting to have it ready for eye duty when required. And I knew it would be required if her body language was anything to go by: she was beginning to sag, to make a round-shouldered retreat, to return to the little girl of her past. But she hadn't quite given up. "I've thought about this a lot recently. I feel you observe me, watch me, all the time, Milan. It's like I'm some kind of experiment you're involved with, and it freaks me out. We're not together, not like a real couple is together. We're separate."

"Who wants to be like other couples?" I appreciated immediately this was a somewhat feeble response, especially when, in all likelihood, it was Bridgette's sole ambition in life.

"You know what you say to me sometimes when we make love?" She looked at me and now there were tears forming in her eyes, being drawn up from that deep emotional well women seem to possess. The handkerchief was being untwisted in preparation for use. "You say, 'Give yourself to me.' You cry it out. You shout it out, so urgently, always so urgently. 'Give yourself to me.'"

"So? That's not so weird, is it?" I wasn't sure, to be honest.

"But it's you who doesn't give yourself to me. You hold yourself back—and all the time, not just in bed."

"But you have orgasms now. And you told me you never used to."

She shook her head. "You don't understand, do you? You really don't understand. It's not about orgasms, Milan. It's about being with someone, the two of us being one. Together. I don't give a damn about orgasms."

She started to cry. I lit another cigarette—it gave me something to do—and I thought: "She should have said, 'I don't give a *fuck* about orgasms.' That would have sounded better, certainly been more literary. I must remember that line." I felt a little sick. I've never been able to cope with women leaving me, I have to leave them. That's how it was supposed to work, that made it more bearable.

"You're after perfection, Milan. Nothing's ever good enough for you. No woman is ever going to live up to your ideals, it's an impossibility. No woman will ever be beautiful enough, loving enough, clever enough for you. It's all in your head. It's all in your imagination. I want someone who'll accept me for who I am."

"Please don't use clichés," I said.

With her head down and her voice gone all quiet and the handkerchief carrying out mopping-up duties around her face, I could barely hear her. When she started again, after a moment's silence spent dabbing her eyes, I had to lean toward her to catch what she was saying. I shouldn't have bothered. "The fact is, our relationship has been very ordinary, nothing special."

Even months later those four words are still burned on my conscience: "very ordinary, nothing special." She'd dismissed our three years together with such finality, summing them up with just four words.

"Well, see how special it is with one of your fucking creatives!" was the best reply I could come up with at the time—and I call myself a writer.

A minute later, when she stood up to leave, her handkerchief still clasped in her hand, I said, "I want my letters back."

She looked taken aback, momentarily lost for words. "But they're mine," she finally said. "You sent them to me, you can't ask for them back."

During our time together I'd sent her many letters. I'm not sure why. I think it was a part of being in love—I told myself it was what lovers did, but it was also a part of how I saw myself—as a writer. A writer should write love letters, that's what writers did. I asked for the letters back because I wanted to punish her: I knew she'd want to keep them, probably to read through in her old age. But I also thought they might be useful to me one day. I might put them in a book. A collection: *Milan Zorec's Love Letters*—no, better to say, *Love Letters*. Milan Zorec. Or maybe just include them in my collected correspondence, possibly a companion volume to my *Rejection Letters*.

"I don't want to give them back. I want to keep them."

I had this rush of hatred, a desire for revenge. I wanted to hit her then, hurt her, smash her complacency and her niceness, and her betrayal. I could see her leaping into one or other of the *creatives'* beds within days. She was pinned against the wall just inside my front door, and I had my fists on either side of her head, our faces almost touching. "I want my letters back. You'd better send them to me, otherwise I'll come round and get them." She had her head down and her hands up to her face and she was crying now, really crying. I was happy I was making her suffer, but I was also, perversely, unhappy that there was now nothing left between us. It had all evaporated. I didn't hit her, and I didn't get my letters back, and that was it, finished, all over between us.

It's late April (I'm not sure of the exact date, and rarely am), and this is the scene that confronts me most days.

The city is covered by a grey mist. The dark cobble-stoned streets shine damply, and the river tumbles between stone embankments and ancient bridges. I'm reminded of a Scottish town. It has the same old-world feel, like something out of a Victorian novel. Probably it would be more accurate to say it's a city from the end of the Second World War, a Dresden or a Berlin. It's almost impossible—unless I look toward the outer suburbs—to see any building that's remained untouched by the bombardment. Like soldiers returning from the front, heavily scarred and with limbs missing, or bandaged carefully in a vain attempt to stop their guts from falling out, the faces of the skeletal buildings are gouged by shrapnel and bullets, complete walls have disappeared, and windows have been blown away and replaced with plastic sheeting. They could fall at any time.

Packs of scavenging dogs are the only creatures at home in these surroundings. Like a flock of birds in the sky, the pack swings this way and that, ebbing and flowing, keeping perfect formation as it casts first one way then the other for prey, wheeling and swooping through the deserted city streets it now rules. Sometimes, if there are no people around, a sniper will pick one of them off, out of sheer boredom. When this happens, it's interesting to note how the victim's companions scarcely break their stride. There might be the smallest of hesitations, as if they were saying, "Oops, Rover's caught it!" but then they continue on their way. If they react at all, it's to run faster, as though to distance themselves from their unfortunate friend. They return eventually, when they think it's safe to do so, to claim the victim, having carefully studied the body—their dinner—for some time from the end of the street, doubtless with much salivating and rumbling of stomachs.

When I was young—I don't remember what age, but under ten for sure—I would build pyramids with other boys, usually of stones, cans, or bottles, and sometimes all three, and then stand a certain distance away—this had to be agreed on by all of us and strictly adhered to—and we'd proceed to throw rocks at this edifice. Having constructed it, we then attempted to knock it down. Always it ended the same way: with each boy creeping closer and closer as the pyramid crumbled before our onslaught—a whoop of triumph greeting every direct hit—until, at the end, we'd be standing on top of the site trying to smash the last rock, can, or bottle from point-blank range. It wasn't possible to knock this lone object off anything because it was the last remaining one and was already lying on the ground. The fun lay in pulverizing what had already been weakened. It struck me the other day that this is what we're now doing to Sarajevo. There's barely anything left standing, so we're just trying to flatten what's already been flattened. We're like kids jumping up and down on a mound of dirt, screaming with glee, throwing bombs and bullets instead of rocks at the dust at our feet, trying to destroy what has already been destroyed.

Skeletal people, certainly short of food and possibly starving, dressed in dusty, dirty rags, wearing shoes made from strips of carpet or pieces of wood, continue to go to the wells for water and to their offices for work. I ask myself why they don't give up and leave. For that matter, why don't we give up and leave? I've only been here a few weeks, but already this siege strikes me as pointless. I don't say this to the others because I know they'd disagree with me—*they* are having a very enjoyable time. So long as I continue to gather material I guess I'll stick it out. If that's what the besiegers of this city want to do, and if that's how the inhabitants of the city want to live, good luck to all of them. I'll continue to jump up and down on this pile of rubble with them. I'll continue to destroy everything in my path. It's mad, but like most madness it has a certain appeal.

I think of Dante. Abandon all hope, ye who enter here. And I wonder at which level of hell we are living here.

Today, for the first time since I arrived here, the sky is a brilliant blue. The weather is definitely getting warmer. There are still cold snaps, and at night it's usually freezing, but sometimes, during the day, weak sunshine spills like a Turneresque watercolor across the sky. The snow and slush have been replaced by grass. The green startles. There are buds on the trees up in the mountains, and every now and again I see a smattering of flowers—no, an *explosion* of flowers, an explosion of color that matches the explosions in the town. Crocuses and cyclamen, primroses, and blue flowers whose name I don't know are scattered among the trees. Nature, I've noticed, doesn't make any sound around here. With the almost incessant sighing of shells overhead and, a second or two later, the *krrrump!* as they hit their target, it has taken me a while to realize this. It's as if Mother Nature has been shocked into silence by the shelling, regarding the events happening around her with dumb stupefaction—unlike me. I feel at home in this noisy bedlam, quite accepting of the outlandish lullaby.

Even the cemeteries that litter the city landscape have taken on a refreshed, resurrected air. It's possible, with spring almost on us—maybe already here—that those who lie there have found new hope and may soon rise from their coffins in jubilation. They're the lucky ones, I guess, those in the cemeteries, because corpses are now being buried in the main sports arena. The playing field, like a badly made bed, is a mass of bumps. Today I'm shooting from the Jewish cemetery high up above Grbavica. The irony doesn't escape me—I lie among the dead and attempt to add to their number. They are my allies, my friends, we are on the same side. The dead provide excellent cover: the grass clusters at the base of the white, smooth stones like pubic hair around a penis. The tombstones lie skew-whiff, as if the bodies lying beneath them have stirred in their sleep and pulled their blankets out of place. The sounds of the mortars whistling overhead, from the wooded hills behind me, and the explosions from the streets below are muffled by the mantle of death under which I sit. I'm writing this resting on a grave at the back of the cemetery, beneath a tree that grows alongside a high brick wall.

The cemetery is on a steeply rising hill. Halfway up the hill is a memorial to the fight against fascism from 1941 to 1945. The white marble slab has a black band around its middle. It's the perfect sniper's resting place, in both senses. Directly below me, across the Pale road, are higgledy-piggledy houses of every color: pink, white, yellow, stone, orange, blue, and green. Few roads run from the main road down to the river, and those that do are steep and winding.

I've been telling my neighbors lying quietly around me about the novel I bought at the airport. I thought it might interest them, but it doesn't seem so. The novel has many pages about the planets and stars, about the universe, about astrology and astronomy, and I've been trying to work out the relevance of these planetary paragraphs. I believe Amis is making a link between the cosmos and this nebulous, hard-to-pin-down information, whatever that might be—although I suspect it's man's awareness of his mortality. His book could therefore be about the place of literature, of man, in the universe, and about whether the writer receives or does not receive this information, this information, which is everything and nothing. When I asked members of my reading group if they'd like to discuss this particular point, they snorted derisively. I took that as a no.

The Information is good. I study and think about the plot. On the surface the book is about literary success and failure, and about the humiliation of novelist Richard Tull. The latter has to suffer the success of his friend, also a novelist, Gwyn Barry, just as I have to suffer the success of Martin

Amis. He's eaten up by envy, just as I am. Creating the plot wouldn't have been too difficult: it's simply the story of two writers, one with talent who's unsuccessful, and the other with no talent who's successful. The writing is masterful, the descriptions, metaphors, and similes—the way it's all tied together in a rich tapestry of words—are typical Amis. He pleasures his readers on every page.

The book is excessive—but of course, can Amis be anything but? That's what makes him so enjoyable to read. The author is angry, an angry, middle-aged man, still raging, still ranting, delivering artistic, beautifully phrased tirades against anyone and everyone. In that respect, Richard Tull must be his surrogate. This character despises everything and, with the exception of his wife, possibly everyone. He could come to Sarajavo, take up sniping, and immediately feel at home. The place would fuel his hatred and anger in a most satisfactory manner.

I tell all this to my neighbors, the Cohens, Baruchs, Fursts, Gluckseligs, Brankos, and Engels who once lived in this city, but who now lie quietly at my feet and never say a word. It seems they're not interested. They certainly have no opinions to offer up. I suspect they must be bored—dead bored. They'd make good publisher's readers.

I, of course, lie at the feet of Mr. Martin Amis, whose father—as is well known, was a writer of some distinction— even went to the extraordinary length of getting the word "art" into his son's name. This Martin Amis—why didn't his parents simply name him Art?—doesn't know that I exist, yet I know him so well. I also know that he's a published writer and I'm an unpublished writer. That's the main difference between us. He has a public, and I have none.

I'm dazzled, nevertheless, by his book. It's so well written I'm in awe. I continue to skip back through it to reread passages, to check what I've already read against where I'm up to now. I want to understand the book and discover the secrets of its construction. I'm determined to miss nothing. Having all the time in the world, I can study the novel at leisure—unless someone puts a bullet in my head tomorrow, which is always a possibility. Hopefully, I'll finish the book before that happens.

His writing is as distinctive as ever. It's clever, good writing. I wonder how easily these metaphors and similes come to him. Does he sit at his desk and write them straight off, or does he have to write them again and again, puzzle over them, worry them—worry *over* them—and try every combination of words until he finds the solution? When he first writes a passage, is it mundane and clichéd, and does he spend a long time thinking about how to make it different? I'd be happier to know he had to work hard rather than discover that such phrases and sentences just rolled off his pen without any thought or effort on his part, purely as the result of inspiration.

Because inevitably, reluctantly, I do compare myself to him. Surreptitiously, even furtively, like men in a public shower, I compare our bodies of work. It's his word against mine, his sentence against mine, his paragraph and chapter against my paragraph and chapter, and every time he wins. He's bigger than me. He has more length and breadth, more bulk. And yet, like him, I build. We're both builders. Words are the building blocks with which we construct or design our phrases, sentences, and paragraphs. I start with three bricks: subject, verb, object. I place one on top of the other and, ho hum, I have a sentence. And it is ho hum—or so the likes of Mulqueeny, the odious Mulqueeny, would have me believe. Whereas Amis starts with the same three bricks, subject, verb, and object, places one on top of the other and has an edifice, a thing of beauty, something of interest that stops people, makes them stare in wonderment, and quite takes their breath away. How does he do it? We have the same materials and yet the results are so different. I'm told that I've constructed a sixties block of council flats, grey, flat, and monotonous, straight out of Brixton, while those supposedly in the know declare that he has built an ornate palace with balustrades, gargoyles, and fancy crenellations, a Brighton Pavilion of words. Mine will be torn down tomorrow, but his will be left standing, if not for all time, then for many, many years to come.

The big story about *The Information* is that he received a £500,000 advance for it. He hadn't even put pen to paper, or so I understand, when some publisher walked up to him and said, "Mr. Amis, we'd like to give you £500,000 for your next book."

"But I haven't written it yet," he replied. (I'm giving him the benefit of the doubt here, trusting he recognized the absurdity of the situation.)

"That's all right, you just hang onto the £500,000 until you do write it."

"But I don't even have an idea for my next book."

"That's fine, old chap. Keep the money, have a good time, go shopping, splash out at the dentist's, just let us know when you have a book ready for us." And the publisher would grovel and fawn (could that be the company name, I wonder) as he backs out of the front door, mightily pleased with his investment.

I understand that only one out of every eight novels will pay for itself, so publishers try to limit their risks by advancing huge amounts of money for just a handful of titles. It works on the theory that the public hears about these vast sums—in fact they're put out there as publicity, as part of the prelaunch hype, virtually shouted from the rooftops—and is so intrigued that it buys the book. The reading public associates price with worth. How cynical is that of the publishers?

And what about all the struggling writers, the ones trying to start out? We're the ones who should be encouraged with substantial advances, not writers like Amis: he's probably a millionaire already, lives somewhere like Holland Park, eats caviar for breakfast, lunches at Langan's, bathes in champagne or ass's milk every evening, and every day, for a spot of fun and entertainment visits either the tennis club or the dentist.

Yes, this is what's truly astounding—it was all over the media, too. He supposedly requires the advance for his teeth. His teeth! What kind of dental work costs £500,000? I admit to having a problem getting my head around this. It was like one of those unbelievable scenarios he's so keen on in his novels—imagination stretching. He was about to undergo major dental work in the US, that's why he needed the money. It's obvious we're not talking fillings here, certainly not a dental hygienist, and I suggest even a crown or two would be unlikely. We must surely be talking jaw reconstruction at the very least. Possibly his whole mouth is to be filled with exquisite, hand-carved ivory from the tusk of an Asian elephant—softer, whiter, and more opaque than the African variety, or so I'm told. I'm ashamed to say I was both fascinated and enthralled, like the general public. It stayed in my head; Martin Amis's teeth stayed in my head. I couldn't get rid of them. I chewed over them. It annoyed me to spend so much time thinking about such a frivolous subject. Frivolous to me, but I guess not to him. Now that I think about it, he's always had a thing about teeth, especially in *Dead Babies*. What was the character's name? Giles Coldstream? He was very funny, a great comic creation, always having nightmares about his teeth and imagining terrible things happening to them. He would imbibe copious amounts of gin in order to anesthetize his mental torment. Perhaps that's how his creator feels.

This fascination with an author's teeth, with the minutiae of his life, means no more and no less than this: our Martin Amis is a star. He's all American glitz and Hollywood glamour. He's red-carpet fodder for *People* and *Variety* magazines, a source of gossip for tabloid columnists. A writer who's a star, now there's a thing. Like a twentieth-century Dickens or Byron. Like Hemingway or Fitzgerald. Not many writers get to become stars, where readers are as interested in them and their lives as they are in their books. Not even readers, just people. People who would never dream of opening a Martin Amis book, nor any other book for that matter— *Sun* readers. They forage for tidbits about his daily life and devour what he has to say on any subject under the sun. It doesn't have to be about writing, it can be about planting petunias in the spring, his favorite restaurant or pub, what he thinks about bringing up children, or his opinion about the merits of pilates. He is a star.

Whereas I am a sniper.

If Art only receives that £500,000 for *The Information* (and the likelihood is he'll receive much more), and the book has 150,000 words—I'm guessing, just to make it simple—then for every word he has written he'll receive £3.33 recurring. He receives £3.33 for every word he writes, while I receive 500 Deutsche Marks (or around £175) for every person I kill. This means he has to write about fifty words to earn the equivalent of what I get for one victim—and most of those words will just be *a* or *the*, *and* or *but*.

It's hard to imagine, even for me, how the people in the city, scurrying through the streets down there, would feel if they were told that each one of their lives, to which they cling so enthusiastically and earnestly, is worth only fifty Martin Amis words. Mind you, to give the man the benefit of the doubt, a Martin Amis word has a certain cachet: few people will understand it and some dictionaries may think it too esoteric to even list. One is not talking here of a common-or-garden *mot*.

Those people in my sights will be more appreciative of my talents, that's for sure. I'm good at sniping, and it's a real craft. It's as much a craft as putting pen to paper, in some ways more of a craft. It's a skill I've become increasingly proud of, and one that I work hard at to make myself even better.

I attempt to bolster my self-esteem by frequently reminding myself of the difficulty of what I do. A bullet spins as it flies through the air. It leaves the barrel spinning at around 2,500 revolutions a second, and the resistance it encounters on its path warps its flight ever so slightly to the left or right. Gravity also does its best to take the bullet off course, pulling it downward. These factors mean that its trajectory is below and to one side of where the barrel's pointing. I must therefore "lay" my rifle, adjusting the sights so that the bullet strikes its target. That is the skill, the artistry of what I do—and could Art do that? The accuracy, the threading of the needle, is absolutely up to me. I like the scientific exactitude of this, the mathematical precision. I like knowing that over six hundred yards, if the calculations are a fraction out at my end, then it will mean the bullet will strike several inches out at the other. I like knowing that. It's not intuition, it's not guesswork, it's fact. It's the difference between putting my bullet in someone's heart and putting it in their upper arm. It's a matter of life and death—for both of us.

When the bullet leaves my rifle, there's a split second—which, at times, can seem like an eternity—before I see the result of my endeavors. If the target is a thousand yards away, which is rare in Sarajevo, it will take the bullet two seconds to travel that distance. It's a long time. I can hum a little tune while I wait, puzzle over a mathematical formula, cogitate on the meaning of life, calculate that to walk such a distance, a thousand yards, would take about sixteen minutes. Sometimes I'm acutely aware of waiting and wondering: I study the targets, still holding my breath in order not to move the rifle, eager to see how they're going to react to the little lump of lead that is speeding toward them, the angel of death of which they're still completely unaware. They're oblivious, utterly oblivious, of the second most important thing that will ever happen to them in their lifetime. Usually they react the same way, like marionettes whose strings have been suddenly jerked. They throw their arms up, their legs buckle, or their head snaps back. Sometimes this is done in slow motion, like a solo dance movement captured on film, full of poetry and beauty. They can be inspiring, as well as enjoyable—even entertaining—to watch, these death throes. Always, it seems to me, the people I shoot appear puzzled. It's strange. Perhaps they're unable to understand why this particular mishap is happening to them. "Why me? Why has God called me so suddenly, so unexpectedly? I was convinced I had a few more years."

If I'm fortunate, the quarry doesn't buckle to the ground immediately. That can make for a disappointingly short show. I prefer it when the person stays upright for a moment or two, possibly taking a step this way or that, as if pondering his or her fate, or simply reluctant to leave the stage. One of my targets reminded me of those opera singers who go through a whole aria after they've been mortally wounded. He staggered backward and forward along the street for what seemed like an eternity, doubtless watched by a few fellow performers in the wings, wide-eyed, their hands to their mouths, waiting to applaud this bravura performance. He collapsed, finally, into the gutter. Most of my victims, however, tend to exit the stage quick smart, in a suburban, amateur dramatic kind of way.

That's how I remind myself how good I am.

I dreamt about your teeth last night. You must be on my mind.

I was in a fairground, at one of those sideshows. It was a shooting gallery. There were other galleries to my left and right. The target was a beautifully carved, intricately ornate, painted face mask. It was larger than life-size. It was your face, Martin Amis's face, with the finely chiseled features, the greased, always wet-looking hair swept back from the high forehead and the intense, faintly disdainful, almost sardonic expression frozen forever. But instead of your usual serious face—I don't think I've ever seen a photograph of you smiling, but I suspect that is because of some complex you have about your teeth,you were grinning like a madman, possibly even laughing. Your eyes were staring, your irises like marbles rolling in the base of the bowl of your eyes, and your mouth was wide, wide open to reveal two rows of brilliant, perfectly formed white porcelain teeth. Your face was all grin, a crazy grin, like a caricature.

After paying my money to the spruiker—I don't think it was a very high admission fee, I'm sorry to say—I had to shoot down as many of your teeth as possible with the bullets allotted to me. Every time I hit a tooth it fell backward with a satisfying clunk, leaving a black, gaping hole. I was working my way along the upper and lower rows, having a great deal of success—from memory I'd hit a couple of incisors, a canine, and three or four premolars—when the rifle started to shake in my hands. I found it more and more difficult to control. Then I realized I was weeping. I was sweating with the effort of controlling the rifle, which had suddenly grown unbearably heavy, and weeping with pain and anguish. The spruiker, standing nearby, his arms folded across his chest, a cigarette dangling from his bottom lip (he looked a bit like you, too), was regarding me with indifference, or was it disdain? He was dressed in a white coat.

Perhaps he was your dentist? Great sobs continued to well up inside me. How could I do this to you? My body was shaking so much, I dropped the rifle. It exploded as it hit the ground, and I woke up. In the distance a mortar was fired.

Outside it was pitch black. It could have been the end of the world, or at least how one imagines it, and I could have been the last person left on earth.

Earlier this evening, I was sitting by the campfire writing my journal, when Stevan joined me. This man is not like other people. A normal person will walk up and sit down next to you, or approach with a smile and a cheerful greeting, but Stevan's much too sly for that. He likes to circle his prey, waiting for the opportunity to sidle up unseen. My guess is that his suspicious nature makes him worry that exposing himself to view too soon may mean his overtures (the most repressed *overtures* I've ever witnessed) will be repulsed before he has a chance to put them in motion. Instead, he lopes around his prey trying to look as if he has other things on his mind, as if he has absolutely no desire to sit down next to you and chat. And then, when you're least expecting it, he swoops.

He sat hunched up next to me, almost lying forward on his knees, taking quick, furtive glances in my direction with increasing regularity. He's a weasely individual with a quivering, ratlike nose, which he continually wipes with the back of his hand. Finally he spoke. "What are you writing?" He was staring at the open journal on my lap.

"About my experiences," I answered. "That's what I'm thinking of calling it: *Experiences*."

"I hope it is favorable to us?" He laughed nervously, but continued to study my reactions with sidelong glances.

"Of course it is. Why should I write anything unfavorable when I'm fighting on your side?"

"That is true." He said it without conviction, perhaps indoctrinated in the idea of no one in the world having anything good to say about the Serbs.

I should be more careful. Although not too many people here speak English—and among those who can, even fewer can read English—I must be careful my journal doesn't fall into anyone's hands.

"You can tell the world about Tudjman and Boban. Not enough people know about them."

"I'm not writing this for publication, Stevan. It's only for me. It's like a diary. But tell me, what should the world know about those two men?"

"They have killed hundreds of thousands of Serbs and thrown them out of their own homes. Everyone says how bad we are, but the other side, they are much worse, and no one says anything. Look at what happened at Pakrac and Ogulin. Many Serbs were slaughtered in those places. People should be told about that too."

He took another of his sneaky looks at me and, grinning broadly to reveal a fine array of blackened, crooked teeth, launched off on a completely different subject, as if the slaughter of his people no longer concerned him. "I am going up to the farmhouse." And he quickly, almost instantly, put on a tired, satiated air, in exactly the same way that a man will choose a certain necktie in the morning to let the world know how he feels. He wore this look blatantly, proudly, as if he wanted people to clearly understand where he was off to, what he was going to do when he got there, and how it would affect him.

"Good for you," I said. He contemplated the ground at his feet, or possibly his coming exploits in the farmhouse— it was hard to tell—and we lapsed into silence. I closed my journal. I wasn't comfortable writing in front of him.

There's a lot of talk every night about this farmhouse. The men talk about it more than they talk about the city they're besieging. It's where they keep the women they've captured, the young girls and wives of their enemies. Rather than being brought down to the battery or to the camp, they're kept locked up in a big farmhouse on the edge of the village. They come from distant places, new areas captured by the rampaging Mladic. Some of them are no more than girls, from what I've heard, most of them Bosnians and Muslims.

Many of the men go up to the house after they've eaten, some before, just as men in England will visit their local for a leisurely pint before or after their Sunday roast. There's another group that goes up to the farmhouse every night, and sometimes even during the day. They're the hardcore group. They relish every moment of their visits and afterward love to recount their adventures in endless detail—half of which I fail to understand—to anyone who'll listen. There's no shame to be found there, quite the opposite. They're mightily pleased of what they've done and boast openly of fucking, buggering, or being fellated by the wives, mothers, daughters, and sisters of their enemy—quite possibly a woman who only recently lived right next door to them.

I suspect some of the men are in the war only because it allows them to visit the farmhouse. If I mentioned the word "patriotism" to them, I think they'd wonder what I was talking about.

Nikola, the one who claims to be a lawyer, wandered up at this point. He addressed Stevan: "Is he coming with us?"

Stevan shrugged. He turned to me. "Do you want to come to the farmhouse?"

I answered no. "I'm tired," I explained. Like Nikola, I addressed this remark to Stevan. He'd become a kind of instant go-between.

Nikola laughed, and said in his smarmy way, "A man is never too tired for that."

He was trying to play the part of a man, or how he imagined a man to be, and he wasn't being too successful, or not in my opinion. It was too obvious he was playing a part. Although he was holding himself like a cowboy in a western, I was only able to see the lawyer with a bumbag around his stomach. I shrugged.

"They have some new ones up there," he said, now addressing me for the first time. "They were brought in today. It's good when they're new; you know that every man and his dog have not been there already."

I still refused. At the time, I didn't bother to ask myself why I refused to go, but I think it was something I wouldn't be happy to either observe or take part in. Also, I dislike Nikola. But now I think that maybe I should have gone, just for the experience. Everything should be of interest to me here, absolutely everything. That is why I'm here.

Stevan was particularly puzzled by, or suspicious of, my refusal to accompany them to the farmhouse, and asked— much to Nikola's amusement—if I liked boys. He said they could get me boys if they were more to my taste, and I could see that he was talking about himself. He leant forward, half his face crimson from the flames, his nose twitching in the half-light, and suggested that, because there were no boys, I could use the women like boys. I pushed him away and said no. He frowned at me, then shrugged, feigning indifference.

Nikola said something to Stevan under his breath that I didn't catch. They both laughed, staring at me and nodding their heads. I asked him what he'd said. "Nothing." He was grinning. I insisted, and there was a sudden, expectant silence, as if the men around us could sense the possibility of trouble. But Nikola was so pleased with his little joke he repeated it to me anyway. "I said that you are more interested in reading books than fucking. That is all."

I said nothing. There didn't seem any point.

"Reading books and writing in your notebook," he added. Although I've made no effort to hide my notebook from anyone, I was surprised. He saw that. "What are you doing—spying on us?"

"I'm fighting for you, Nikola. How can I be a spy?"

He sneered. "I don't believe you are here to help us. I think it's because there's something in it for you."

"What's in it for me?"

"I don't know. I haven't worked that out yet." And a moment later the two men went off and left me in peace.

Can you be left in peace in a place like this?

I stare down at the city from my hiding place. Going round in my head are the words, "If you can see the hills, the hills can see you." I'm told it's how they think down there, those citizens of Sarajevo. It's drummed into the heads of schoolchildren and office and factory workers like a lesson in road safety. "If you can see the hills, the hills can see you" is a warning against snipers.

It works both ways, of course—or that is what I suppose: a good view of the city means a good view of the hills or the Grbavica apartment blocks across the river. There could well be a sniper in position, watching, waiting for my muzzle flash. In a book I read before coming out here, it stated that the enemy will have an idea where a sniper's shot came from to within twenty or thirty degrees and one hundred yards. So firing that first shot is a little like waving a flag and shouting "I'm here, I'm over here."

Before the UN became involved, there was much less likelihood of anyone shooting back at us. There was usually just the one enemy, probably a civilian, so as long as you hit your target, they weren't going to retaliate. But snipers are becoming more numerous in the city now, and certainly there are enough for me to know that I can't afford to be careless.

I now understand why we receive 500 Deutsche Marks for each victim we kill. There's the danger of enemy snipers, yes, but claiming a victim is also not as easy as I thought it would be. On some occasions it's particularly hard. What's strange is that there's no system for proving a kill: they simply take our word for it. Such trust, in these surroundings, in this chaos and with these people, is absurd. It seems out of place, especially when there's so much room for error. Mordo, the man who used to shoot at his brother and sister-in-law in the city, told me it's been calculated that, in one week, over nine hundred people can be hit by our snipers, but it's usually only a little over a hundred of those who are declared killed. One in nine doesn't seem a high success rate, until you consider the challenging circumstances. There are the easy ones, of course, the suicidal ones, those who, with pig-headed obstinacy, amble across the road or down the street as if they were strolling along Oxford Street on a Sunday afternoon. They at least allow me to scratch another notch on my rifle butt. I can thank them for that. I can now feel the notches against my cheek when I raise my rifle, and the number is reassuring. The marks on the rifle butt show I've left my mark on the city, and it's not yet the end of May.

Most days I kill.

I look at the statement, which I wrote down with scarcely a moment's thought, and I'm stunned. "Most days I kill." That "I" is me, Milan Zorec, school janitor, would-be writer, son of Pavle and Betty Zorec, British citizen. I wrote that. And if it's true—which it is—then the fact that I kill on most days means I've become a mass killer—no, *not* murderer, killer. There's a difference. I kill, I don't murder. I simply do whatever I do on a large scale. These kills, my victims, the people behind the notches on my rifle butt, are scarcely known to me, but I do sometimes make an attempt to imagine their lives so that I can feel I know them. I want to know them, it feels like it should be part of my task. To be involved with these people, to take an interest in their lives, is the least I can do. It's important if I want to be a writer. You can't avoid people if you write books, that's the truth of it. All novels are about people, so I can't suddenly stop taking an interest in them, however much I might want to at this moment in my life.

The only changes in my daily routine are the locations I choose and the weather. I like the fact that every morning I choose where I go to work. Now that the days are warmer,

I like to leave the dirty, dusty apartments and head up into the hills. Often I sit among the trees and write this journal, smoke cigarettes, or simply stare into space and think. I may not bother to shoot at all. It's like a holiday, a spring or summer holiday. Sometimes I lie on the grass, my eyes closed, basking in the warmth of the sun on my face and feeling the pulse of the earth beneath my back. For the briefest of moments, I can almost believe that life is good, perhaps the best I've known. It can be a real effort at such times to find the motivation to get up and go back to shooting people.

I find myself less keen to write about my victims now, to even think about them or their lives. Having always literally been distant to me, they have now become distant to me figuratively. I'm removed from them. I look at them through my sights, but they don't come any closer. They're magnified by the scope, but still remain distant. I'm forced to keep a tally of the number of kills, so that I can later claim my 500 Deutsche Marks (paid directly into my bank account in London), but I now notice that I have to make a note of each victim immediately it happens, otherwise, at the end of the day, I find myself thinking, "Was it three I killed today, or two, or maybe four?" It's sometimes almost impossible to remember, they blur together so.

People's lives do blur together when you play God: they become too small and insignificant to bother about. I'm aware of this tremendous, Godlike power I possess. Real power, more than a headmaster, a CEO of an international corporation, or even a publisher will ever possess, more than I have ever known before. With an almost imperceptible movement of my finger, so tiny, so insignificant that even God might miss it, I can choose to snuff out someone's life—or not. The power of life and death. Possibly it is no different to how a publisher feels about the would-be authors that pester him every day. "Was it twenty manuscripts

I rejected today, or fifteen, or maybe thirty?" Neither of us feels any guilt, I'm guessing. For both publisher and sniper, it's a job, routine, the only people who may get a little upset are the rejected author and the wounded citizen. Or the wounded author and the rejected citizen.

I reread a letter I'd received from my mother. She, too, has become distant, as if I'm looking at her through the wrong end of my rifle scope: she's decreased in size and importance. It's not even as if I miss her. And the letter, her letter, bored me, that's the truth of it. It was inconsequential, as if she wanted to avoid saying anything that might cause a reaction. She's been living with Dad too long, and maybe she thinks I'm no different to him. That would be something. I almost threw the letter away, but told myself not to. If I want to be a writer, I should study it. I should be able to copy her style. It's all grist to the mill, or whatever the expression is. And what is grist, a grain or something? I miss my dictionary at times, most days in fact. I miss books, full stop. I imagine wandering down into the city in front of me, down to the main library to spend time in its reference section, or among the novels and biographies. The library's gone up in flames, so there seems little point in such idle speculation.

Writing has always been an effort. It's painful. Having my toenails pulled out would be a welcome alternative; to die of the Ebola virus, seeping blood from every orifice, would be a relief. When I'm confronted by the blank page, I suffer. And yet, despite the suffering, despite everything, I have always dreamt of being a writer. It's all I've ever thought about, a thought that's been with me every moment of every day; my religion. The truth is, writing's been a part of my life for as long as I can remember. I mulled over plots as I mopped the school corridors, puzzled over what motivates a character as I walked home in the evenings, tried to decide on the importance of various scenes as I cooked myself a meal. I'd wake up in the middle of the night and write an idea or a line in the notebook I kept by my bed. People talked to me, but I didn't hear what they said; they waved to me in the street, but I didn't see them; they stopped in front of me, but I walked right past them. Writing involved me body and soul. Sometimes it caused the outside world to cease to exist.

Many times Bridgette accused me of not listening to her and went home in a huff because I didn't give her enough attention. And it was all, this total absorption with writing, with one aim in mind: to be published. Yes, I know people say that once you've achieved your goal in life, no matter what it is, you won't be satisfied. I don't believe that. If I walk down Oxford Street one day and pass a Waterstone's bookshop and in the window see my novel—hopefully even several copies of it—I swear I'll be happy. I'll be in heaven. Being published will give meaning to my life, to an existence that increasingly strikes me as being without meaning. It's all I've ever dreamt of, all I've ever wanted. To see my name in print has always been my sole ambition.

It's my destiny to write, that's what I feel. It's why I'm here on earth, as well as in Sarajevo. It may have taken Van

Gogh thirty years to get around to realizing that he wanted to be a painter, but I've wanted to be a writer from the time my mother started reading me bedtime stories at about the age of three. I remember sitting on the bed, snuggled up next to her, her arm around me, as I listened to her quiet, soothing voice. And the point I'm trying to clarify, sitting here now against the bare wall of an apartment in a deserted city in a foreign country, is that I remember those stories. They continue to give me comfort even today, they are what's important. And when I was little, leaning against my mother in bed all those years ago, I thought I'd like to write stories such as those. Whoever wrote the stories, whoever magicked me away to strange and wondrous worlds—through wardrobes or down rabbit holes—was clever, and they made me want to be like him or her. Imagine making up a story, weaving all those words together into a tempting trap in which to catch a reader. To hold power like that over another being and make them follow your path, your will, that would be quite something. I thought, when I grow up, that's what I want to do. That feeling has never left me. It is part of my being, an ever-present dream. And for a time—certainly when I was young—it was my mother's dream too. She encouraged me, in her bookish way, to be a writer, to pursue my dream. And I think she did so because she believed in me, that I would succeed. It was only many years later, I'm not sure when, that she stopped believing in the dream and started to try to encourage me to follow more conventional careers. I think my father had finally won her over to his view, and she then deserted me.

All the books in our house were my mother's. And they're still there, fiction mainly, but also biographies, poetry and nonfiction, on shelves that line every room. Most of them were bought from library sales or at secondhand bookshops. They were all dog-eared, with broken spines, loose pages, and worn edges. In the front they sported ex-libris and library stickers. Few had covers, and those that did were torn or had pieces missing. The margins of many were covered in my mother's notes in pencil or biro, and often had whole paragraphs underlined; most of them were from her youth. Only rarely in my life have I held a new, spotless first edition, and when I did their unblemished state and special smell, their purity and originality, made my heart beat violently with excitement. It was a very precious thing.

It's strange that my father was never seduced by the thousands of volumes that he walked past every day. The house was, and still is, more like a bookshop in Hay-on-Wye than a home, and it touched me, influenced me, but never him. For me, it's a museum of my reading history. Those are the books that have shaped me from when I was young. I read many of them again when I was older. In my youth I read *The Wind in the Willows*, *Alice in Wonderland*, *Robinson Crusoe*, and *Tom Sawyer* . . . I could tick them all off. When I was older I read Tolstoy, all of his books, and Dostoevsky, just some of his. I read bits of Dickens, lots of Shakespeare, most of Jane Austen, Goethe, Mann, Joyce (but neither *Finnegans Wake* nor *Ulysses*), Balzac, Zola, and Flaubert. Some of these books were borrowed from the local library, others came off my mother's bookshelves. I read many when I was far too young and didn't fully appreciate their artistry. I'd put *Crime and Punishment* and *Madame Bovary* into this category. I thought I was being adventurous in my reading at the time, but looking back now I see that it was nothing but conservative. They were the books one was expected to read. I didn't venture far off the well-trodden path of the classics.

Zen and the Art of Motorcycle Maintenance, *One Flew Over the Cuckoo's Nest*, *Catch-22*, *The Naked and the Dead*, *Steppenwolf*, *Confessions of Felix Krull*, *The Counterfeiters* . . . Those are the titles that come to mind now, but the list is endless, as are the shelves on which the worn, well-read ("much loved" is probably what they'd say today) books gather dust. These are the books that have touched my soul in the past and now accompany me through life. They've left an indelible mark on my being and influenced my every thought and action. I haven't read them, then put them away to forget them; I haven't been able to. They've stayed with me.

I've read modern authors, too, like Banville, Proulx, Updike, DeLillo, Bellow, and, of course, Amis. I've read all of them, and some of that talent and artistry must surely have rubbed off on me. I can't have been impervious to it, can't have been immune.

My mother has always been a great reader. The fact that my father has never read at all possibly explains why he's so bigoted and narrow-minded. It's obvious to me now, in Sarajevo, that he's typical of his countrymen, unable to see any point of view but his own. He's little different from Santo in that respect, who, after I'd been in Sarajevo only a week, told me with great enthusiasm how the Serbs had bombed the majestic, Egyptian-style National Library with incendiary grenades for three days—three whole days. "Two million books went up in flames," he said. "You should have seen it, Milan. The sky was black with ashes. Sheets of burning paper floated upward, blotting out the sun, then descended like black snow." He let his hands drift through the air, his fingers piano playing to some wintry tune in his head, eyes wide with the wonder of the scene. "It was like confetti falling on a newly married city."

He gave his machine-gun laugh, as if embarrassed by his eloquence, his hands settling onto his lap, while I wondered where the metaphor had come from. It surely can't have been his.

"Now they have no history," he said, "now they have no past. Without that, they cease to exist."

At that moment I think I truly hated Santo. I wanted to shoot him.

Mordo, sitting on the other side of the novel hater, periodically and vigorously rubbing his bald head, leant forward to say to me: "It was Nikola Koljevic who ordered us to destroy the library. He's Karadzic's deputy, but he is also our most famous Shakespearean scholar. He's a professor, and much respected in academic circles. What do you make of that, Milan, a writer destroying all those books?"

I could make nothing of it at the time. It was beyond my comprehension. I was disgusted and, the more I thought about it, horrified. I imagined my mother's reaction. She, also, would have been appalled, and doubtless disgusted to see her son sitting around the fire with such men, talking to them like old friends. She'd have hated them and their ignorant vandalism —perhaps me too, now.

I wondered if Amis's books had been in the library— translations. It was possible. Along with all the rare manuscripts which the library doubtless owned, his words would not have survived. His ideas would have gone up in smoke, disappeared from this part of the world, his art expunged.

Mordo, giving me the quickest of glances, as if he thought it would be rude to stare for too long, added: "They burnt their own books after that. They did our work for us. Now there's not a book left in the city, except for those they've used to build shelters, to stop the shrapnel. Books are good for that, to stop shrapnel."

"They burnt the books to heat their homes," Santo explained. "Mainly novels," he added, winking at me as if I'd find this news particularly amusing. But I felt sick. Hearing those words, the proximity of the men who'd helped perform the deed and were now telling me this tale—yes, it was a story about the murder of stories—made my stomach turn.

"And after they burnt all their books, they burnt all the trees," said Mordo. I could tell he was excited because he was rubbing one of his hands across his bald head, backward and forward, as if trying to build up enough friction to also start a fire. "They have little else to burn now. They have burnt everything." And he threw a small branch onto the campfire as if to emphasize their deficiency.

From those ashes, from those blackened pages, I told myself, a work of art would arise—mine. I'd show my father, whose pessimism dogged my life, whose lack of belief in me killed my every dream, how wrong he'd been. Nor would I disappoint my mother.

I will write, I can write, I'd succeed in doing a Martin Amis, even if I haven't got the word "Art" buried in my name.

Forests at night, I feel, contain men who howl in their sleep and then do Everything. It's everything. Just primordial. Or something like that . . . Staggering out of the slime, with bulging eyes, shuffling gait, long arms swinging loose from barrelled chests, the lackwits, lackbrains, lunatics emerge blinking into the moonlight, to wreak havoc on civilized citizens.

Avram stood before me, grunting who knows what, scarcely able to control the vowels and consonants that dribbled messily, like diarrhea, in streams and spurts, from between his rubbery lips. I suspect he'd had four or five too many—at least. His baggy khaki trousers—an attempt at a military disguise—were tucked into army boots, so dirty, scuffed, and uncared for as to turn any self-respecting sergeant major apoplectic. Barely embracing the vast overhang of his stomach was a grey T-shirt, which appeared to double as a mechanic's hand cloth, so stained was it with oil, dirt, and grime. A hawklike nose and deep-set eyes dominated his loose jaw, clouded with several days' stubble. I remembered that he was the man who'd come up to Santo and me on my first day in camp, long ago. I wondered if, as before, he was going to stand before me and fart. He gazed in my general direction, unfocused and unseeing, as he extended his invitation. Stevan and Ranko, a psychopath, had also sidled up to stand silently before me. It was a delegation from hell, stepping forward out of the flames of the campfire, inviting me to the devil's playground.

Why I agreed to go with them to the farmhouse that night, when I'd refused on so many other occasions, I don't know, nor do I care to question my motives too deeply. Perhaps it was simply to find out what went on up there. Perhaps it was because I was suddenly overwhelmed by the number of people in front of me—for the lawyer, Nikola, realizing that something was in the offing, had also joined our little gathering. Radomir, the man who once trained to be a priest, also attached himself to our party as we left the campsite. I was a little surprised. He smiled at everyone. He was so relaxed and chatty he could have been setting off with friends for a picnic. I wondered if he knew where we were going. Did he think we were simply going for a walk in the woods? Did he believe we were going fishing? It seemed unlikely when we had no rods.

It was a calm, clear night. For a moment one could imagine there was no war, it was so quiet and peaceful. There was a canopy of stars overhead. The trees didn't stir. Lining either side of the path, crowding in, pushing tentacled branches out toward their timbered friends across the way, they watched us pass in silence. The moon illuminated the well-trodden path with a white light. Each man in the group was alone with his thoughts, imagining, perhaps, what pleasures were about to come his way, and how he would satiate himself. They were all led by their lust, like dogs straining on their leads. Nikola held a bottle of beer, which he raised to his mouth at regular intervals, as though oiling the machine that kept him in motion. He was quiet, even by his standards. He had retreated into himself, like the rest. He made a comment now and again as if to maintain standards of politeness, and once told a joke that I didn't understand. The others barely turned toward him when he spoke, and said nothing; they were in a different world. Suddenly Nikola hurled his empty beer bottle at the black wall of trees that lined the path, and it exploded against a trunk. This display of violence momentarily stirred his companions to raise their heads and snort approvingly.

See, now, the next day, I write "his companions," as if I were not one of them. I didn't feel one of them, that's the truth. Even there, even then, I was an observer, an outsider, scarcely part of the action. If this means I'm an author, what then? Who's writing my life, who's writing my story? Who set me in motion along a path at night, near Sarajevo, through a forested blackness, with men of ill repute, toward a house of infamy?

Nikola started to sing. It was a song unknown to me. His voice was weak, high-pitched. It seemed out of charac- ter for him to break into song. One could scarcely imagine him warbling in the shower. His showers would be practical: a quick soap here, soap there, a cursory shampoo, rounded off with a bracing, healthful, tap-full-on, cold deluge. But there was no escaping the fact that he was singing. Ranko and Stevan joined in, the latter sidling into the lyrics in much the same way that he progressed along the path: obliquely, attempting to be unobtrusive.

Avram, to my astonishment, then performed a little jig. And it was little—abridged, transitory, extemporaneous, like a flash of out-of-character behavior that he could no longer contain. He took half-a-dozen steps, lifting him- self briefly onto his toes before falling ponderously back to earth, causing his stomach and breasts to rise, then fall, like a jackhammer in the street, three balletic blancmanges in perfect harmony. I felt moved and privileged to witness such a performance. Radomir laughed good-naturedly, and patted Stevan in a friendly way on the back, as if they were outside a church on a Sunday morning and sharing a joke after the service.

As our group progressed toward the old farmhouse, this singing and dancing lapsed, then died out completely. The effort had exhausted our giant friend, and the lawyer showed no enthusiasm to perform alone. Ranko was dan- gerously silent. It was important they all preserved their strength: they had strenuous exertions looming ahead in the gloom. So they stopped dancing, they stopped singing, they concentrated on breathing. For the giant, that was enough exercise. "Stentorian" was the word that sprang to mind. His breathing was stentorian.

Approaching the farmhouse, there was little light. From within curtainless windows I saw flickering candles. It could have been a church at Christmas; carols wouldn't have been out of place. Some of the windows downstairs were covered in cardboard, but many were uncovered, as if the occupants in the house didn't give a damn who walked up and peeked inside, or because they wanted everyone to know what was going on. But there was barbed wire too, great rolls of it all around the house, situated a few yards from the building itself. There was no sound of celebration or laughter from inside. I expected laughter, the clink of glasses, the sound of animated chatter, but there was only an eerie silence, an oppressive, uncanny silence, as if the house were empty or abandoned.

Outside the front door, there was a guard. He didn't seem to take his job too seriously. His rifle lay at his side, and he was sitting on an upturned milk crate, smoking a cigarette. He barely looked up as we approached, although he acknowledged Avram in much the same way that a waiter in a restaurant will acknowledge a regular customer.

The door opened and we were sucked into the maelstrom. It enveloped us, drew us in like a woman, the door closing behind us like a vulva. It was dark, *noir*. Shadows and candlelight. There were candles everywhere, on the floor, on mantelpieces and window ledges, on the edge of the stairs, on the few pieces of furniture. Between the candles there was deep gloom, the impenetrable gloom of a black hole. Who'd gone to all this trouble? It was as if someone had intended to make the setting romantic. What was it about candles? Black masses, devil worship, virgins spread on marble altars surrounded by hooded, robed, and menacing men. But also found in churches, white and pure, before the statue of the Virgin Mary. They're adaptable, candles, that's for sure. But why not electric lights? Too bright, too all seeing, leaving no shadows into which one could retreat and hide, was that it?

What I remember most was the smell. A rank odor. Of sweat predominantly, but also sex. Like the warm smell between the sheets of a couple who have just made long and passionate love. But there was no love here, no love at all. This was fucking, rooting, rutting, not the coming together of bodies, but the clash of animals in the wild, not commingling but brutal separation. This was subject and object, dominator and dominated. There was also the smell of alcohol, and something else, which at first I couldn't place but, later in the evening, realized was the cloying smell of blood—or was it death?

My eyes had a problem penetrating the gloom. There was penetrating going on all around me and me, I was having problems penetrating the gloom. It was amusing, kind of. People moved from light to shadow, some clung skulking to the shadows as much as possible, as if reluctant to show themselves, and some moved brazenly in the flickering light. It was like viewing some old camera obscura, frame by frame, the images jumping and, at times, hard to discern.

What did I see? The images from that night also flicker and die, indistinct, interrupted, indecent. There was sound, but not very much. It came in snatches.

Snatches.

On a table in the center of the room, hard to miss even in that poor light, lay a figure. It was a woman, although not obviously so at first. Her hair was short and black, her face, arms, and hands also black. The rest of her body shone white by contrast. (Many women in this war try to hide their sex from the enemy by cutting their hair short, blackening

themselves as much as possible, and strapping their breasts
flat beneath their clothes. Anything to avoid the inevitable
humiliations and suffering brought on by detection.) She
lay on her back, not moving, her legs hanging off the end
of the table, her eyes closed—although it was hard to tell in
these surroundings, with her face in shadow. For all I knew
she could have been dead, she lay so still. A man, older than
most of us, squat, fat, and balding, with his trousers around
his ankles, stood swaying between her bare legs. He was
pallid, flaccid, drunk. He was attempting to arouse himself,
his hands before him tugging forlornly, even desperately, at
his cock. A younger man, holding a bottle of beer, stood
next to him at the table watching, waiting until it was his
turn. Suddenly he grew impatient and shoved the older man
aside, sending him sprawling onto the floor, feet caught up
in his trousers. The younger man, the bottle of beer still
grasped in his hand, undid the front of his trousers and,
with a grunt, brutally heaved the figure off the table and
turned her over. She could have been a sack of potatoes.
She lay with one arm caught beneath her body, like a discarded puppet. He entered her from behind and she never
flinched. The older man stumbled to his feet, cursed the
figure now engrossed in thrusting between the thighs of
the sprawled, motionless woman, and, pulling up his trousers, made off across the room in search of uncontested
prey. They were like vultures squabbling over carcasses. The
younger man continued about his business dispassionately
with as much feeling as if he were ploughing a field.

It's a man's world, I thought, primeval and stupid, where
brute force reigns supreme. It's a serious world. War allows
men to look serious. It's a serious game, war. When war
comes, the women stop laughing at the men. They're too
scared to laugh then, too appalled. They, the women, know
they no longer count. Cunts that don't count. Men reign in

times of war, and all contact between the two sexes is terminated. Relationships are dead, between man and woman, between man and man. War is a solitary activity, and best carried out alone. Destruction is everything, the name of the game, to kill before being killed. Survival.

Complete control over another human being. Complete and utter control. With no ramifications, no consequences. No one to question what you do, no one to ever call you to account. Everyone else is doing it—it being everything and anything—so what does it matter if you do it too? Santo had said as much to me in my first month here; he'd told me about the anarchy.

What would you do with such complete control? What would I do now if I had Ms. Diane here? Rape, torture, a lingering bloody murder with sharp knives—slicing, prying, picking, pricking—they all spring to mind, and not just for Ms. Diane. Who is to say what you would do, what I would do, without restraint, with no lines drawn, no limits. Don't throw the first stone, that's for sure. Don't set yourself up as being without sin, blameless, because you never know. You never know until you've been there. War never breeds the sanctimonious, that's for sure. We're all the same, not even deep down. We're all the same on the surface, too. And you don't know how you'll behave until you're there, until you experience war. You'll only know yourself when you've observed yourself at times like these. Then you'll understand how complicated people are, how they're often contradictory, always surprising, never predictable.

In the shadows on the other side of the room Stevan sat, hands clutching a woman's matted hair, forcing her face down onto his lap. I walked across and stood over him. He looked up, right at me, but didn't see me. There was nothing sly about him now, no need to sidle; he was a different man. He looked demented, his eyes opaque, a crazy grin on his lips. He had retreated to somewhere deep behind his eyes. He was certainly not there in front of me.

I walked through to another room and saw red-haired Ranko stubbing, stubbing, stabbing his cigarette out on a woman's breasts. She did not cry out, just gasped, almost as if with pleasure, or was it because she was beyond caring, beyond pain? There were marks all over her breasts, they were like wooden ashtrays, seared and sagging. These men had no imagination, so they copied each other. One man had used this woman as an ashtray, and every other man had come along and thought, "Ah yes, that's a good idea. Why didn't I think of that? I shall do the same." And now it was Ranko's turn.

The men wanted to punish. They were here for their own gratification, but they wanted to inflict pain on others while they took their pleasure. That was their pleasure, to inflict pain on others. They were drunk, with alcohol, but also with bitterness and anger. They were beside themselves (beside themselves: where does that come from? Does it mean that they're outside of themselves when they become emotional, standing beside themselves watching what's going on?)—beside themselves with the desire for vengeance. They wanted to wreak havoc, to punish someone, anyone, another, for the situation in which they now found themselves. They were taut with anger, stiff and unyielding. The anger they felt for themselves was vented on another, elsewhere, with stiffened members. It was revenge. On women, on the blameless—*because* they're blameless. Men felt their own suffering and now wanted others to suffer, especially women. Women were to blame for everything. Women were to blame for this, the farmhouse, here and now. It was their fault that they were here. They brought men into the world, so it was their fault they were here. This was no time to be petty, but yes, she was the first to eat the apple, too. Women subjugate men, if not brutally with words, then with tears, with silence, with whispers and caresses, with a look, even by their absence. They're in control, no question about it, the whores. But not now, not here, not in control here and now. This was different. The tables had been turned. Now, they're silent, they have been silenced. In every room I visited, they were pinioned, pinned down and ploughed, impaled by men who were no longer subservient, men who were brutally rampant. Termagants tamed by tumescent men. End of story.

I was in what used to be the kitchen. What were they cooking up here? It was probably the biggest room in the house. There was a fireplace in the middle of one wall, and the logs were crackling merrily. It was too homely, I thought. Men sat around the room drinking, their faces in shadow, their laughter muted. They jeered and leered. Some had women at their feet, discarded temporarily, until they were needed again. The women were all naked, although one or two held a piece of clothing to her breasts in a hopeless attempt at decency or modesty. They sat like Mary at the foot of the cross, inconsolable. They were covered, coated, caked in mucus and slime, like animals, but not of their own choosing. The men were sanguinary, the room sanguinolent. A shriek of pain came from upstairs, interrupting all the sounds of the room I was in. The men looked up briefly before turning back to whatever they were doing. A few laughed, as if the scream might have been put on for their amusement. Two men were dragging a woman up the stairs at the far end of the room. Why bother to go to another room, I wondered. I saw Radomir, beautiful, boyish Radomir from the seminary, seated in a corner, alone, fingering his rosary. He was watching everything going on around him. A cynical, devilish smile on his handsome, angelic face, unaware of me. It's impossible to know someone, I think—

impossible. Impossible for a novelist to create such a character, or at least to make him believable.

Avram, slobbering, pushed a bottle into my hands and beckoned me to follow him. He went upstairs. I could go up there too, I told myself, simply to observe. I could watch. Could there be more to see? I could gather material. It would be research. It would be valuable experience.

I was not a character in a novel, at the mercy of an author, at his beck and call, a marionette of his mind. I was not a fiction, not a figment of someone's imagination. I am the author. I am my own master—that's what I told myself. And I made to follow Avram.

At the foot of the stairs, glimpsed through one of the kitchen doorways, was a woman. She resembled some road victim, horizontal, spread-eagled, and in messy disarray. She was being pulled roughly by some fellow—*manhandled*—but it was as if she was anesthetized against what was going on around her, even happening to her. It was like she wasn't there. What really struck me was that in the split second she turned her head—so fleetingly I scarcely saw her—*she saw right through me*. I wasn't attracted to her or anything, absolutely not. She wasn't even good looking. Far from it, she was old enough to be my mother. It was the way she looked through me.

It was then I decided to walk out of the farmhouse and head back to camp. No one saw me leave, but that didn't bother me. I was happy to be by myself.

I'd seen enough.

Santo is beginning to bore me. In that respect also he's like Mulqueeny. Just now, lying on his bunk across the room from me, he said. "Why did you not ask me to go to the farmhouse with you?"

I'd sensed that something had been bugging him. "You weren't around."

"Why did you go with that arsehole Nikola?"

"He was one of many."

"We're friends, aren't we? And friends do things together."

It strikes me more and more that the man's a fake. He doesn't believe in what he's doing. He's too easily swayed by those around him, and everything he does—the sniping, the visits to the farmhouse, even his joking around—is all an act. I've seen his sort in the school playground: they go along with the other kids because it's easier than standing up for their own beliefs. They pretend.

"We are friends, aren't we, Englishman?"

He sounded pathetic, but I was tired. I answered, without conviction, "Yes, sure."

A strange pastime I indulge in sometimes—*another* strange pastime of mine—is to go through the list of famous authors who have been rejected. They're an elite club, of which I, also, am a proud member. I find it encouraging.

Watership Down was turned down by over twenty publishers. *The L-Shaped Room* was rejected time and time again, as was Lampedusa's *The Leopard*. *The Commitments* was returned by so many people, Roddy Doyle eventually published the book himself—and it went on to become a best seller. *Gone with the Wind* was rejected eighteen times, as was—probably correctly in my opinion, *Jonathan Livingston Seagull*. *The Naked and the Dead*, one of my favorite novels, was returned to its author by no fewer than twenty publishers. Stephen King's first five novels were all rejected, including *Carrie*. George Orwell (*Animal Farm*), James Joyce (*Dubliners*), D. H. Lawrence, Patrick White, and even the great man himself, Count Leo Tolstoy, were all rejected at some time in their lives. Agatha Christie's first novel was rejected by about seven publishers. She was supposedly so demoralized that she almost gave up. And in one of the most unbelievable mistakes of the modern era, William Golding's *Lord of the Flies* was turned down by around twenty (that magic number again) publishers.

Those are just some of the novels on my list that weren't recognized when they were first put out there on the market. There are many more. Those dismissive publishers must now—hopefully—be spewing with envy, self-loathing, and regret. They'll be tearing their eyes from their sockets for being so shortsighted. And they'll be doing the same because of me one day. "Why didn't we spot Zorec's talent? It's so obvious now, with hindsight. How could we have made the mistake of sending him so many rejection slips?"

I read an article recently in which a publisher mourned the good old days. He said that once it had been possible to judge a novel from the first page, but now, thanks to the proliferation of writing schools and creative writing courses, it was necessary to glance at a few more pages. He found this irksome—that was the word he used, irksome. "Everyone has a modicum of talent," I think was the way he put it.

What's important is that I find my own unique voice. And I'll find it here in Sarajevo. The sniper novelist hasn't been done before, and that's what will make me stand out. In a world gone crazy for novelty, peopled by the mentally deficient for whom the first page of a novel has become the equivalent of the ten-second sound bite, I will deliver.

Once I hatched plots to trap literary agents and publishers, like everyone else, from what I've heard. Should I leave a few blank pages after the first page? Should I insert an incredibly rude or crude message a few pages into the manuscript? Or a bribe? Should I insert something that they simply couldn't ignore, which would tell me whether or not the manuscript had been properly studied?

I also imagined typing out a few pages of *War and Peace*, along with a synopsis of the plot, then submitting it to see if the manuscript was rejected. I considered doing the same with *Hamlet* and *Ulysses*. More to the point, if those books had never been published and were submitted cold now, today, would they be accepted, or would the authors simply receive a standard rejection slip? "Thank you for your submission, but your manuscript doesn't fit with our current list." Maybe those particular submissions would be deemed of sufficient interest or merit to justify the inclusion of a few encouraging words with the rejection slips.

"Dear William, Your *Hamlet* is interesting, but is it realistic to have the protagonist kill his own mother and his uncle? Our reader also has concerns with the number of bodies at the end of your play: four altogether, with another two offstage. It doesn't make for a happy ending, and our readers do like happy endings."

"Your novel (entitled *War and Peace*) is a most interesting story, but we have no place for historical novels on our list at present. (See attached submission guidelines for your future reference.) Also, to be perfectly frank, we find your novel has too many long-winded and intrusive digressions about philosophy, agricultural management, politics, and religion, which we feel hold up the flow of the story. We suggest you delete some, if not all, of these sections, as you would then have a more marketable novel."

"We're sorry, but none of our readers could understand your novel, *Ulysses*. (What are you on, do you mind us asking?) It might also prove a worthwhile exercise if you were to learn the basic rules of punctuation—especially toward the end of your book, where you seem to have given it up completely. We suggest you might benefit from investing in a copy of Strunk & White's *The Elements of Style*."

No, I'm not comparing myself to Tolstoy, Shakespeare, or Joyce; just making a point.

The publisher's reader, that's the one I blame. What does he know? He sits in his musty bachelor pad (I'm incapable of imagining a reader having a partner), surrounded by manuscripts. There's a general air of poverty about the place, resulting from his perpetual struggle to earn a crust. The study area is dilapidated. At one end of the cheap secondhand desk is an old computer, while at the other end a pile of unread manuscripts overflows onto the threadbare carpet. In the middle is an ashtray full of butts. The reader's own manuscript, his baby, the ugly fruit of his withered loins, the bastard on which all his hopes rest, incubates in the computer.

Novelists manqué shouldn't be doing this for a living. They shouldn't be allowed to see the novels of their rivals.

They shouldn't be invited to pass comment, let alone criticize, the progeny of their competitors. What are they going to say, *what*? That this man is such a talent, much better than they, that his plot is excellent, his writing masterful, and they're generally in awe of his ability? Is that what they're going to say? I think not. They may believe this, but they're going to keep it to themselves if they do. Their mean little conniving, scheming minds will quickly work that one out. "Why should I assist him? Why should I give him a leg up when I can't get published myself? Why should I hold out a supportive arm when all I get is rejection slips? Why should he be favored, instead of me?"

A reader is more likely to help himself to my ideas than to help me. Imagine reading a manuscript that has a great idea in it, a really good, original plot. If the reader chooses to reject it, even better, chooses to be scathing about it, and if—which is likely—he doesn't see the book ever show up in the bookshops, he could pinch the idea for himself. Why even wait a couple of years? Why not change it around immediately: rewrite some of the characters, alter a few of the situations, put it all into his own words, and send it off to a publisher? Who could resist having that put down on a plate in front of him? Certainly not a cunning, two-faced, frustrated, bitter, and twisted reader, that's for certain. They'd be onto something like that quicker than they could burrow up a publisher's backside.

On 28 June, we celebrated the most important, if not the most sacred, day of the year in this part of the world: Vidovdan. It's in honor of the Battle of Kosovo back in 1389, when the Serbian kingdom was defeated by the Ottoman Empire. Today Milosevic still raves against the hated Muslims for the defeat at Kosovo six hundred years ago as much as he raves against the hated Croatians for siding with the Nazis just fifty years ago. Those are his twin justifications for all of this, for the siege, the war, the murder and mayhem. It's revenge, no more, no less.

If there's a higher interest, a worthwhile cause, can that be made to justify everything? These men hang onto their higher interests like little flags they wave in the air as they head off to slaughter their enemy. But are the people they're fighting even the enemy? Some of them are attempting to slaughter their friends, some their own families, but if they're carrying their little flags it doesn't seem to matter. The slaughter itself is their raison d'être, this higher interest is their excuse.

It was strange to celebrate a defeat, but after endless glasses of Slivovitz, and barbecuing a whole pig over the fire, it did begin to seem sensible, natural, possibly even desirable.

I was also celebrating—without telling the others—the release, after several weeks, of some UN peacekeepers, among them some British men who'd been used as human shields by Radovan Karadzic to prevent further NATO air strikes on Pale and Gorazda. I'm not aware of feeling any allegiance to my country of birth, so was puzzled that I felt any pleasure at their release. I'll have to try to work that one out.

Despite all the camaraderie, the dancing and singing, the campsite is one of those crowded places that somehow manages to throw into sharp relief the solitariness of man.

I'm very aware that just to the north, on the other side of the hill, barely visible against the night sky, is a city, also crowded, silent and black, hiding in the darkness from us, making us feel even more secluded than we do already.

It certainly tends to dampen my feelings of jubilation.

Early this morning I crawled to one of the apartment windows facing the city. I suspected I'd be the only sniper in position at such an hour. With luck I might catch a careless citizen out collecting water or bread, one of those who trusted that every Serbian sniper would still be asleep, nursing a Slivovitz hangover.

As I slowly raised Gilhooley—also up early and, as always, enthusiastic and keen to get down to work—above the window ledge, he was suddenly wrenched out of my hand and flew, doing a complete somersault, back across the room. I stared at him over my shoulder: the top of his head had been blown off and his dark glasses lay skew-whiff across his woollen face. I was shocked. As for the headmaster, he looked traumatized, possibly dead.

"Mr. Gilhooley, are you all right?" I whispered. Inching my way back from the window, I picked up the stick on which his head had perched, also the damaged balaclava with articles of clothing now protruding from it. "Thanks, Gilhooley. That could've been me."

"I wish it had been," he said in his usual supercilious tone. He sighed. He sounded as if Fate had dealt him a poor hand.

Were those to be his last words, I wondered? It was certainly typical of him to be so self-preoccupied at such a time, not sparing a moment to consider my feelings, my miraculous escape from Death's embrace. I grinned nevertheless, relieved that he was still alive. But he was in a bad way, with half his head missing and his pulse weak, if not nonexistent.

For a moment, I contemplated leaving him where he was and running up- or downstairs, to a different room to see if I could spot the enemy sniper, but my heart wasn't in it. If someone was now targeting me, as Santo had always warned me would happen if I became too successful at sniping, then perhaps it was better if he thought he'd killed me. So I sat outside in the corridor and had a cigarette. Later I patched up Mr. Gilhooley, who was still moaning and carrying on in a desperate bid for sympathy. His brains, full of blackboard ephemera, useless history dates, the names of boys and girls and teaching rosters, I stuffed carelessly back into his cotton skull. "You should live," I said. "Don't go on about it."

It happened when I was in prison. Definitely, that's where I had my *epiphany*—if that's not too grandiose a word. I remember staring at the grey walls and bars that enclosed me, the bars discolored halfway up their length by the thousands of hands that had gripped them over the years. That's when it first struck me that I should go to Sarajevo. It was suddenly so obvious and clear: I would escape.

As I lay on the hard, stained mattress trying to block from my consciousness the snores of the two men sharing the cell with me, I looked up at the dim night light outside in the corridor and remembered what my father had told me at Christmas about the city among the mountains where he'd been born. I knew I'd be welcomed with open arms, just as he promised. They needed me as much as I needed them. I was so excited by these nocturnal musings, I was sorely tempted to wake up the more educated of my two cellmates and inform him of my decision. But wisdom prevailed.

In the early hours, it dawned on me that I should go to Sarajevo for the experience. That was my sacred duty as an author: to experience life, to record those experiences, to follow my instincts, to surrender to every impulse. So that's what I'd do. I'd become a sniper. It didn't sound too dangerous. The citizens of Belgrade were rumored to go to Sarajevo for a weekend of sniping—for fun. It had a certain frisson about it, but without too much risk. I could then collect material for a novel that wouldn't be boring, plodding, or expected. I'd write a book that Mulqueeny's reader would be incapable of saying was predictable or he'd read before. It would be different—so different it would be unique. I'd find a story in Sarajevo that hadn't been written before. In that nightmare city I'd fulfil my lifetime's dream, discover an idea that even the slowest, stupidest publisher's reader would be unable to resist.

There was no place for me in England, that was for certain: I'd reached a dead end there. The place was like a stagnant village pond overgrown with duckweed. The place was boring, grey, and predictable. I needed change. Not only was it likely I'd feel more at home in the country of my father, but it was likely to be a more valuable experience than cleaning out the school toilets. Like Stephen Dedalus I would choose "silence, exile, and cunning."

Looking back I think the ordinariness of life in London was reflected in my writing, and I had needed to distance myself from the mundane. The London I knew was cold and wet. Just before I left I had lived—no, existed—through those miserable January and February days when the realities of life quietly reassert themselves over the abstractions of Christmas and New Year; when the celebrations, joviality, and bonhomie surrender once again to the weary, humdrum, crowded trudge to work. A continuous stream of cars and double-decker buses splashed through the wet streets of Kilburn, while crowds of people jostled and dodged each other on the pavements. The area concentrated hard, did everything in its power, to be rundown, dirty, and *brickish*. In that suburb I felt perpetually bricked in; it was like living life in an unplastered room. Anything green—and there was very little that was green, apart from the baize inside the local snooker hall—had to fight for air, for space, just like the people who lived there. Restaurants, like overflowing rubbish bins, spilled along the pavements: Caribbean, Indian, Turkish, Thai, burger bars, as well as the halal meat shops. Discount furniture stores battled with cut-price supermarkets' betting and charity shops carried on their uneven fight for people's dole money; and outside one poky, begrimed shop, suitcases were lined up, padlocked together by a single chain, as if promising a possible escape to a brighter, greener, less brickish place. The incessant noise (as omnipresent as the smell of curry) numbed the brain, the honking, droning, rattling forever in my head.

Little wonder I was struggling to write something different, something that had never been seen before, that was truly original. It had been necessary to escape, I can see that clearly enough now. The only excitement in my last year, the only moment of originality in that dull metropolis, the only event that sticks out in my mind during those twelve months of nothingness was the time I returned to my flat in the early hours of the morning, when the traffic on Shoot Up Hill was only spasmodic, and found the Dawes' cat, Sharon Stone, hanging from the wrought-iron corbel that supported the lintel above the main door, mouth open as if she was still keen to inhale a little oxygen. Slowly turning in the darkness, she resembled some highwayman of old, on a gibbet at a crossroads on the moors. Bridgette stood next to me on the front doorstep at three in the morning, screaming beneath the gently oscillating body, like some demented Janet Leigh in the shower—*Janet Leigh discovers Sharon Stone*. And I remember thinking to myself, "Well, Milan, this is a bit more exciting than usual. This is a little different. This is nice and neighborly."

The last two days have been busy: the enemy tried to break out of the city. As people say: "It's easy to get into Sarajevo, impossible to leave." There was some heavy fighting, and for a time it was more exciting than usual. Just what the doctor ordered.

They started to bombard our positions to the east and west of the city soon after dark, but it was a pitiful display. I wouldn't have noticed anything different if someone hadn't told me what was happening. They have no heavy firepower down there, although there are rumors of American-made assault rifles and antitank weapons now getting through. After they'd fired at us for about an hour, convoys of trucks, the leading ones laden with soldiers and followed by others full of huddled civilians, made their bid for freedom. There was something frenetic about it all, a desperation accentuated by the crashing gear changes and laboring engines of the trucks. After our cannons found their range, there was also plenty of shouting and screaming. The scene was lit up by exploding shells and the flicker of flames. Across the sky, phosphorescent tracer bullets stitched haphazard paths. Some people tried to escape from the disabled trucks, and we picked them off as they ran for cover at the sides of the road. We caught a few of them, but in the poor light it was difficult to tell how many. Many trucks were abandoned, some bursting into flames. A few succeeded in turning around and heading back to where they'd come from, bolting back to the safety of their holes.

It struck me as a particularly futile exercise, and I couldn't even see the sense in us retaliating—apart from the fun of doing something different and breaking the monotony. Why not simply let them flee the city? If a few people escaped, so what? If everyone left, what did it matter? If they had succeeded in breaking out, where were they going to go? They didn't have the manpower to surround us, that was for sure. So they'd have been faced with a long drive through territory that we hold, with little prospect of reaching their own people. We'd be able to pick them off one by one. It was, like most aspects of this war, quite pointless, but also momentarily entertaining.

"Life being what it is, one dreams of revenge." That was Gauguin, the accountant-cum-artist-cum-lover-of-natives fellow. And my spokesman.

Yes, I was upset. She upset me. It was that simple. So I planned to fuck her up. I dreamt of doing a Gauguin on her. It would be the perfect way to get at Mulqueeny, by getting at her. I wanted to laugh at her. Hand up to my mouth, mimicking her pretence of stifling the guffaws, I wanted to laugh at her humiliation. But how best to bring this about, that was the tricky bit.

The choice was between psychological and physical damage—with the latter striking me as possibly more satisfying. The problem with psychological damage—poisonous letters, anonymous phone calls, whispered innuendos, and suchlike—was that the results were too hidden, too hard to quantify, whereas with physical damage there was the satisfaction of surveying broken legs, smashed hands, bruises, possibly even a permanent limp—the latter obviously providing me with many years of pleasure. On the other hand, rape is the first thing that thrusts itself forward to the front of one's mind when one thinks of getting at women. They supposedly consider it worse than being killed. The problem is, I'm not sure that I'm up to it, being totally honest with myself, not sure that it's up my street, my bag of tricks, my *thing*. Paying someone else to do it might be just as satisfying, so long as I could watch. Some Corleone lifted out of the phone book, or maybe listed in the Yellow Pages under GBH. There again, it might be more fun to be the instigator of the damage. To follow her home from work one evening might prove most satisfactory.

Watch her leave Mulqueeny's office. See her walk against the stream of traffic and the dancing glare of wintry headlights. And, as I'm sure she does every evening, make note of how she stops at the post office to hand over a pile of

A4 envelopes, her little recyclable carry bag chock-a-block with recyclable manuscripts—oh yes, we know all about those! She takes a short cut through an ill-lit Soho alley, past flashing strip joints, warmly beckoning bars and restaurants, newsagents and betting shops, on the way to the underground. The pavements, like the roads, are crowded, and sometimes one or other of us has to stop or step out onto the road to let people past. I follow close behind her. It's quite safe: she's too caught up in her own little life, in her own miserable nine-to-five existence, to bother to turn round. She has that young person's walk I hate so much, with the arrogant, thrusting, you-keep-out-of-my-way movement of the body. I hate her cockiness, her look-at-me superior air, and the confident, almost flamboyant way she holds her cigarette. Even that annoys me—smoking in the street. It's so common, so typical of today's young girls.

I enjoy her being unaware that I'm so close behind. She's oblivious to the fact that I'm hunting her, bent on bloody revenge. I anticipate the look of shock on her face when finally I reveal myself.

We join the throng heading down the steps into the tube—it would be Tottenham Court Road, which is close to her office. She walks down the escalators, and I follow her. She goes to the Northern Line platform—obviously. I walk slowly past her, between where she's standing and the edge of the platform. It's a kind of test. I keep my head turned away as if I'm studying the posters on the other side of the track. My stomach muscles are cramping with excitement, like I'm some teenager about to come in his pants. When the train arrives, I get into the adjoining compartment and stand near the door. I keep an eye open at each station when we stop.

At her station, I follow her toward the exit, keeping

her long black hair (which, I have to admit, I'm attracted to) always in sight over the heads of other passengers. She crosses the road to the bus stop. I stand a few yards away, but she never looks round. She gets onto the first bus that comes along, and sits downstairs. I sit upstairs where I can see the mirror showing the platform. When she gets off at her stop, I'm ready. I'm down the stairs and off the bus just as it starts to move away.

I let her walk a little ahead of me. I feel great, really powerful, and I want to beat my chest and send a war cry through the city jungle. I can do anything I want, and she can do nothing—she's powerless. There's no traffic around, and no people. Her heels sound loud on the pavement, an irritating, metronomic clicking. I speed up so I can catch up with her. My rubber soles don't make a sound. It's exciting to move in for the kill when she's so unsuspecting, so blissfully unaware.

It's dark—of course, absolutely. The street lights are lit, but the lights are far apart, so it's suitably threatening. I'm walking right behind her now, right on her heels. I could reach out and touch her if I wanted to, but I'll wait until the time is right. Although my shoes make no sound, she senses me there quickly enough—women hate it when men walk right behind them, I've often noticed that. She slows down hoping I'll pass. But I don't pass. I slow down, too. She half looks over her shoulder, but not directly at me, not into my face. Then she veers across the road, wanting to get away from me.

Her heels are clicking louder and faster. I cross the road too. I can hear her breath. Now she starts to panic, like an animal sensing the hunter closing in and feeling helpless. My heart's going faster, too, but only because I'm elated. I stretch out my hand and touch the top of her hair, all silky and black. She whimpers, but doesn't turn round. I think she's too scared to turn round. She's walking fast, almost running. To slow her down, I grab a fistful of hair and stop. She's almost yanked off her feet. I whisper her name—"Ms. Diane."

We're near a street light, but that doesn't bother me. She can't ignore me now, not any longer. With a kind of strangulated moan, she manages to half turn round. She gasps when she sees my face. Yes, oh yes, when she realizes who I am, when she recognizes me, how can she not gasp? "Oh hello," doing her best to make everything sound perfectly normal despite the fact I've got a handful of her hair in my fist. She knows the situation is far from normal. I say nothing, just stare at her. I think she's mesmerized, like a rabbit transfixed by a fox. I let go of her hair.

"Can I help you?" She forces a little smile, but it's a pretty feeble effort. "I didn't know you lived round here, Mr. . . . I'm sorry, I've forgotten . . ." She's still into ellipses. It's a bad habit, especially for someone working in a literary agency. She needs to be taught a lesson.

I still say nothing. She's clutching her handbag to her chest as if it will offer her some form of protection. Her eyes are wide, and there are tears there, just beginning to appear in the corners. She can't move she's so frightened. I think it's because I say nothing, that's what freaks her out. I like that. I smile, although it's probably more of a smirk. I'm really quite pleased with myself, with things running so smoothly. I don't think it reassures her, my smile or smirk or whatever it is. It probably makes her think I know something she doesn't, and that it's not very nice. She's right. She can obviously be quite perceptive at times.

My next move might be to step forward, right up to her. She'll then back away. Yes, I can see it: up against a low garden wall with a hedge above it. There would be no lights on in the house behind the wall. I'll move against her, just touching. She'll be half turned away from me now, cowering, head down, bowed, panting, almost sobbing. I'll say nothing. Silence is good, that's definitely the way to go.

"I'm sorry, but it wasn't my decision."

I'll still say nothing.

"I'm sorry, truly I am. If there's . . ."

I'll still say nothing.

"You have to believe me . . . It wasn't anything to do with me."

Someone turns into the street. He's at least a hundred yards away. I see him out of the corner of my eye. It's someone walking a dog. Where on earth did he come from? Who thought of introducing him suddenly? But it's too late to object now because she's seen him too. She gives a small cry of hope, the little gasp escaping from her mouth like an upraised hand. But he's still too far away to be of any assistance to her. I place a hand on one of her breasts. It's very firm and young. I squeeze it hard nevertheless, yanking her back to face me.

"Please don't. Not that."

With my other hand I squeeze her throat, raising her onto tiptoe, almost lifting her off the ground. She's making strange gulping sounds, looking down her nose at me, screwing up her eyes as if she's afraid I'm about to hit her. My face is only inches from hers. She's not so confident now.

This is what I'll say, and how I'll say it. "You." Her mouth is a scarlet bridge. "Should." Black mascara, like the dots and dashes of Morse code, runs down her white cheeks. "Be careful." I can feel her breath against my face; sweet breath, still innocent and fresh, despite the tobacco. "Who." I let go of her throat and she lets out a small cry. "You laugh at."

It comes out word perfect.

Then I'll turn and walk off. She's lucky someone came along (why did I imagine that?). I don't know how it might have ended up otherwise. I don't turn back. I make sure I look indifferent, casual as I walk away, as if I don't care one way or the other. Only when I reach the corner do I glance back down the road. She's collapsed on the pavement, huddled up, like a pile of discarded clothes on a bedroom floor, not looking back at me at all. The man with the dog is running toward her, the dog yelping excitedly, pleased that its evening walk hasn't turned out to be as boring as usual.

Of course, as soon as I run that little scenario through my head, I worry that I hadn't gone far enough with Ms. Diane. I tried to think of other possibilities. My revenge should really have something to do with words. Mulqueeny had rejected my words and she'd laughed in my face. Kafka immediately sprang to mind—but of course! His short story about an apparatus that writes on the victim's body whichever commandment it is that he's broken, that would be perfect. But how could I go about finding such a machine? It would be difficult. Maybe I could get someone to build one for me—that bloke in Willesden Green who built my bookcase? I'd be able to set it up in the yard at the back of my Kilburn flat, next to the clothesline and rubbish bins. But the thought of having Mrs. Dawes out there all the time, complaining about the state of her hubby's legs, asking me what I was doing and could I keep the noise down and where was Bridgette and who was this new one, this Diane, made me think it might be better if I came up with another idea.

On 11 July the Serbs (maybe I should be writing "we"?) captured the UN-declared safe areas of Srebrenica and Zepa. In camp, everyone had a good laugh. We jeered at the United Nations, and declared that these towns were now really safe, now that *we* were in charge. The celebrations went on long into the night, but left me strangely uninvolved. I don't give a damn who ends up in charge of this country—although I'd never tell my father that. He wouldn't see my point of view. Who wins and who loses, who cares? The country isn't worth conquering now. Whoever takes over will always be looking behind them, wondering if they're safe, because none of the factions will ever get complete control. They'll only be able to rule, retain their grip on power, by suppression. In ten or twenty years time there'll be another war, to right some of the wrongs of the past, to even things out again.

I think I hate them all. If I had my way I'd put the lot of them up against a wall and shoot them. That's what they deserve. The Christians and the Muslims, the Social Democrats, the Communists and the Liberals, the Serbs, Croats, Bosnians, Hungarians, Macedonians, Montenegrins, Albanians, and Slovenes, they're all as bad as each other. Maybe I don't give a fuck who I shoot now, friend or foe, it's all the same to me. They'll just be another notch on my rifle butt, another 500 Deutsche Marks in the bank.

After the battle of Srebrenica, it seems there was a massacre—of Muslims. I don't know if it's true, but that's what people are saying. What I do know is that the Serbs marched into the city as victors, whereas here we just sit in the hills and shoot into empty streets. It's not a battle, it's a siege, and I'm beginning to wonder if I should move elsewhere, to where there's proper fighting. But then I ask myself if I want to die for some cause I don't believe in. If I'm simply searching for a story, then it's probably better that I stay put. No idea on earth is worth dying for, surely? Is it?

This afternoon, after lying motionless for hours, I decided I'd had enough for the day. I moved my head fractionally back behind the tree so that I could crawl out of sight and rest. There was a puff of air, a crack as a bullet embedded itself in a tree just a few feet behind me. I froze. I remained low, hugging the ground, my face in the grass. I watched a tiny insect crawl over the obstacles of leaves and twigs that blocked its way. Although scarcely breathing, I was thinking quite dispassionately about how that was the closest I'd ever been to being dead. I must have avoided death by a millisecond or so. I even put a hand up tentatively to the side of my head to check if there was any blood.

As I lay there, I remembered the man who'd walked up to me in the camp a few days earlier. "So, Englishman, you are still alive?" he'd said.

The man had stood before me, his hands in his trouser pockets, legs apart, looking down on me as if I was some trapped animal he'd stumbled across on a tour of his estate and which he hadn't expected to survive another night.

"I'm sorry to disappoint you." I was sitting by myself on an upturned packing chest waiting for Santo, who'd gone across to the kitchen area to collect his food.

"Not for long. You won't disappoint me for long." It was said matter-of-factly, without any sign of malice.

"What's that supposed to mean?"

He stared glumly, at my chest rather than my face, possibly trying to work out in his own mind why I hadn't yet been killed, then turned away without answering my question. I almost went after him, but decided not to waste my time. It was for him to worry about, the fact I wasn't yet a corpse, not me.

But now he'd almost been proved right.

I was a little surprised by how relaxed I felt about this incident. I wondered where the shot came from and how long the sniper had been watching me. I imagined he must have seen me move into position—over three hours ago, because I'd have been hard to spot once I was in position. I also wondered if the sniper had been aiming specifically at me, if, as Santo once suggested, my signature had now been recognized? Possibly the shot had been totally random: I was simply another enemy sniper. I thought that was more likely. I was more concerned I wouldn't be able to move safely for at least an hour, possibly until dusk.

Back at the Vraca camp, when I mentioned to Santo that I'd almost been killed, he told me to be more careful. I was moved by his concern, but only briefly. A second later he added, "If you are shot I will probably lose that army coat I gave you."

A minute later he was telling me word had come through that the Croatians had launched an attack on Serb forces in the Krajina region of Croatia, southwest of Sarajevo. "There has been a cease-fire down there for several months, but now it seems to be over. This is good, this is what we want. The only reason people arrange cease-fires is so they can break them, and now that has happened we can get back to fighting again."

Two days later there was a repeat performance, this time in one of the Grbavica apartments. There was again a rush of air next to my head, so close, like a *crack!*, then a two-second pause before I heard the distant bang from the rifle. Two seconds meant he was two hundred yards away, and that was too close. The bullet hit the wall behind me. There was a small crater in the masonry that hadn't been there a moment ago. It would have been a massive hole in my head. So much adrenalin surged through me, I felt queasy. I wasn't so much annoyed with this stranger (I'm convinced it's the same person now) who's trying to put an end to my life, I felt more like he was someone I was playing chess against. It had become an intriguing problem. I had to deduce his next move as well as work out a counterattack. I wanted to win this game.

This experience—being shot at and almost killed—will prove invaluable in the future. So long as I survive. It's a dream scenario for a writer: "He risked death to bring you the horrifying reality of life in the frontline." That kind of thing.

Santo wasn't around this evening, so I was able to take advantage of his absence to approach Radomir. I'm not sure why I preferred to set it up with him. Perhaps it was because he'd once studied to be a priest and therefore I trusted him more. It's a little weird if that was the reason, but who knows. Maybe I just remembered how upset Santo had been not to accompany me to the farmhouse, and I felt like upsetting him again.

The next morning, early, Radomir and I went to the apartment block in Grbavica. It was pitch black. I guided him to the room I'd been in the day before. I wasn't concerned using the torch. It was unlikely anyone would see us, but if they did, so much the better. I offered to leave Gilhooley with him—stimulating, educated company for his long wait—but he said he'd brought his own decoy, so the headmaster accompanied me. We arranged for Radomir to make his move at ten. We checked our watches. "Be careful," I said.

"God bless you," he replied. I almost did a double take, wondering if he was being ironic, but he didn't seem to be.

I headed back downstairs on my own soon after five.

There were red and white blocks of flats, three stories high, with balconies front and back, a hundred yards up-river from where I left Radomir. They were shaped like boomerangs, the two end ones concave toward the river, and a middle one convex, with each building slightly overlapping its neighbor. They were perfect for my plan. As I walked there, I was careful to keep a building between myself and the river, just in case there were any Bosnians already up and watching. It didn't seem likely at that hour.

I chose the farthest building and went up to the second floor. There'd been a fire inside and the walls were pock-marked with bullet holes. Cautiously I raised Gilhooley above the window ledge . . . Nothing. I lowered him and then took a look myself. I had a perfect view of the building where I thought my sniper friend was hiding. It was a little to the west of the main railway and bus stations, and looked like some kind of power station covered in tiles, with four small windows—more like portholes—at the front, plus half-a-dozen ventilation outlets. I could see that enemy snipers had been inside before because the porthole at the bottom of the structure was scarred all around by bullet holes and the tiles had been dislodged to reveal the bare concrete underneath. It seemed like a good place to hide, the building isolated in the middle of a large patch of derelict land. Bricks, sheets of corrugated iron, weeds, and rusting railway equipment lay everywhere round about. The railway line, now disused, ran directly behind the building.

I retreated to the back of the room, opened my thermos flask of coffee, and lit a cigarette. I was nervous, but it was mainly excitement. I felt I was hunting someone, and I liked the feeling. Hemingway said something about the hunting of armed men being the best kind of hunting there is, and once you've had a taste of it you never want to do any other kind. And he was a Nobel Prize winner!

I prayed that the sniper who'd been preying on me hadn't moved, that he'd grown complacent. I was hoping that having enjoyed some success from this position, and doubtless including me in his kill total, he'd be persuaded to stay put.

At nine o'clock I moved into position and set my sights. Gilhooley sat beside me. He was holding his breath, not talking at all. He was excited, I could feel it. After all, this sniper had blown a hole in his head and almost killed him. He wanted revenge too.

The minutes ticked by slowly. Just before ten, I was tense with concentration. Radomir was about to raise his decoy in the building farther along the riverbank. I stared at the tiled power station. Suddenly there was a muzzle flash— not from the building at all, but from beneath a sheet of corrugated iron lying on the waste ground immediately to the right. I caught it out of the corner of my eye. No wonder I'd had problems tracking this sniper. I moved my rifle ten degrees, lined up the gap between the corrugated iron and the ground, aimed about three feet back from the flash, and slowly squeezed the trigger.

I waited about a minute, chambered another round, and repeated the shot, only this time a fraction higher. Then I retreated from the window as fast as possible and, leaving Gilhooley, who was beside himself with excitement, I leapt down the stairs two at a time and sprinted to the other end of the three apartment blocks. I knew it would be more directly opposite where the sniper was situated. I ran up to the first floor and, acting totally unprofessionally—because I was pretty sure I'd already killed my friend—I threw myself carelessly down by the window and fired another shot beneath the corrugated iron from this slightly different angle . . . and then another. Then I waited. I waited an hour. There was absolutely no movement, no sign of life. This didn't mean much. I knew that if by some miracle the sniper had survived our trap, he wouldn't attempt to move until after dark. But I was fairly confident he wouldn't be moving anywhere. At worst, he'd be severely wounded and bleeding to death.

I met Radomir back at camp. We congratulated each other on our successful mission and drank Slivovitch together. We ended up having a bit of a chat.

"What did you do before this happened?" I asked him, even though I knew the answer from Santo.

"I was studying to be a priest."

Although I pretended to be surprised, it wasn't so difficult to imagine him saying Mass, being kind to old ladies, and blessing children. I also knew that for the villagers in this part of the world, there were really only two options if they wanted to avoid a life of poverty and hardship: to become a priest or to join the army. Radomir certainly looked the part. He was a Botticelli angel, with black curly hair, a peaceful, understanding smile, and startling blue eyes that really did twinkle.

"So why are you now a soldier, and not a priest?"

"I ask myself that question, Milan. It was lots of little steps, I think. There is a time when you are studying for the priesthood, and then a little later you are studying to be a soldier, and you do not even realize you have traveled the distance in between." He shook his head, as if to show he did not understand how the process worked either. "The main reason, I think, is my best friend wanted me to join the army with him. He said I could study for the priesthood once the war was over. It is probably because of him."

"Will you go back later?"

"I do not know. I'm not sure that I believe any longer, that is the problem I have now." And he gave me this broad smile, revealing a perfect set of dazzling white teeth. A minute later he frowned. "Have you heard of the Marquis de Sade?" I nodded, a little taken aback by a Catholic priest raising such a subject. "You know what he said? He said that if God kills and rejects mankind, then why should we not do the same? Those words have been in my head a lot during this war."

I wasn't sure what to say.

"It is true that God kills us, mocks us, makes all of our lives miserable every day, so it is difficult to argue against why we should not behave in the same way. Why should we behave well when He does not?"

"Do you believe He's on our side, Radomir, or on the side of the enemy?"

"I think He is on no one's side. I think He has gone off on holiday and said to Lucifer: 'It's all yours, Lucifer. They do not interest me, those people in the Balkans. I leave them in your capable hands. Do whatever you want with them.' That is what I think."

I couldn't imagine Radomir returning to the seminary after this, after what he'd seen and doubtless done. Yet what struck me very forcefully was his seeming lack of conscience: so far as I could tell he had absolutely no guilt about what he was doing now. He was quite at peace with himself, and had perhaps made his peace with whomever he believed was "upstairs."

"My life was very quiet before this." He grinned, his face open and uncomplicated, totally without guile. "You know the most exciting part of my life before the war?"

"A woman?"

"You forget, my friend, I was studying to be a priest."

"Before that were there no women?"

"A mountain village is not like where you come from. It is many decades behind the times." I nodded. "No, for me, it was fishing. It was feeling that pull on the line when you have hooked a fish, that was the most excitement I had in my life. I am not complaining, however; it was more than enough for me."

"You did a lot of fishing?"

"It was all I did, all I ever wanted to do. Whenever I had time I would head off to my favorite spots by the river. I could sit there for hours. It was like I was in a trance. I did not move. I was happy. Even if I did not catch any fish I was happy. For me, being by the river, that was enough."

Earlier today, there was an incident a little out of the ordinary. I feel bad about it. I don't know what came over me, it was so . . . well, out of character. But I must write down what happened, even though it will be painful to do so.

A mother and her child had been to the well at Bascarsija, in the hilly eastern section of the city. There's a strong Turkish influence there. The district, between the river and the city's main mosque, the Chusrev Beg, is a maze of narrow alleys and small shops. I believe it's many centuries old, but don't know how many. The well is ornate, with an imposing wooden tower set on granite steps, the water collected from scalloped marble pools at its base. It's situated in a cobblestoned courtyard, and would normally be surrounded by trees (although these have now all been cut down for firewood), quaint shops, and traditional coffee shops, called *kafana*. I imagine it would make a popular postcard in peacetime. I've often looked down on the district and thought how much I'd like to visit there, to sit in the shaded courtyard, listen to the trickle of water from the fountain, and watch the locals go about their business. Maybe I'd enjoy a coffee while I read a book or worked on my novel. I spotted the mother and child when they left this well. They disappeared behind some buildings, but I could work out the direction they were heading in and knew they'd reappear about a block away. I waited.

When they came back into view they were hurrying, but not taking any great care to keep out of sight, the woman probably believing the child would be her passport to safety. She was struggling with a large container of water, carrying it with one hand, the other holding her child. She was dragging the child along, trying to get him to hurry, but he was fed up—I could see that despite the distance between us. He probably wanted to run off and play.

I was about to shoot a hole in the container—something snipers do every day just for the annoyance factor—but changed my mind. I didn't want to warn her. So I shot the kid first. Kids are the future, so it's important to get rid of them. No kids, no future, that's what Mladic is always telling us. He was about six, but it was too far to be certain. He was pale and skinny, and had the appearance of someone who had lived underground all his life. He didn't look as if he'd ever stepped out of doors to play in the street. That was likely to be his life, hidden in a dim basement, holed up like a rat, so I probably did him a favor putting a bullet in his head.

The mother continued to clasp her boy's hand as he went down, maybe hoping to hold him back in this world, to stop him from falling off into the void, into the black abyss. But I knew he was dead; I could see it from five hundred yards away. I hadn't messed up the shot, I was certain of that. The mother dropped the container of water and, as she turned toward her boy, falling to her knees beside him, I put a bullet in her stomach. It was an impromptu thing, something I did without thinking. Almost on a subconscious level, it was as if I understood I didn't wish her to die instantly. I wanted her to die, yes, but before she died I wanted her to know that her little boy was dead, that he'd never live the life she'd imagined for him, that her dreams for his future would never be realized.

She lay down beside him, carefully, one hand clutching her stomach, the other grasping her son. She moved gently, as if she was climbing into bed beside him and didn't wish to disturb his sleep. There, in the middle of the street, in the bright sunshine, she cradled his head against her chest, and she could have been giving him a cuddle in bed last thing at night before he fell asleep. I could see she was screaming or crying, or maybe both, though I obviously couldn't hear anything over that distance.

It was at that moment, watching this sad little tableau in the distance, I understood how cruel I was being, how much suffering I was causing the woman, allowing her to agonize like this over her own child, the fruit of her loins, the one she'd suckled, and so on and so forth. The pain must have been unbearable, so I decided to put her out of her misery . . . and I shot her. I finished her off. Then I begged them both to find it in their hearts to forgive me for what I'd done. Amen.

But that wasn't what happened, not at all. That's the problem. It's important to get my story straight, to say what really happened. I'm not writing some piece of fiction here.

So let's start again. This is what really happened.

I shot the boy and I wounded the mother. That much is true, one hundred percent accurate. But I didn't finish her off. That was the bit I made up. The bit about my feeling bad and being considerate enough to put her out of her misery, that never happened. I felt no guilt whatsoever. Instead, I edged back from my vantage point and, when out of sight of any possible snipers, I sat back against a tree and lit a cigarette. I left the woman lying in the street, alive, cradling her dead son, mourning his death while dying herself, while I relaxed and smoked a cigarette. Yes, I knew she'd die soon enough, but that's not the point. The point is, I did not feel any guilt or pain about what I'd done, none at all. Radomir would have been proud of me. I think I was simply attempting to add a little spice to my life by saying I felt guilty, perhaps in the hope of making it more interesting, and to hell with how I achieved this. Now, with hindsight, I'm not certain this is normal. Possibly it isn't. I persuade myself that it's too difficult to worry about things like that, telling small stories: life's too short. Ask that mother lying in the street. But I still have this nasty feeling in my head, this niggling pain, this nagging doubt.

Toward the middle of the afternoon, I crept back to my vantage point to see that the mother was still half lying across her boy, using him like a pillow. At first I thought she'd died, but then I detected some movement. She half raised her head and moved a hand out toward the dropped container. She was obviously thirsty. Scarcely surprising in this heat: so was I. But there was no water in the container. It had all soaked away into the ground. I could have shot her again, but I didn't want to waste a bullet. They're too precious. She didn't die until later in the afternoon, that's when I could no longer see any signs of movement. I imagine the two bodies will be removed during the night, although I don't suppose I'll bother to check in the morning.

I'm writing this now, later the same day, and I'm thinking, this is the kind of story I'm after, the kind of story that should interest me. It's unusual, a little off-the-wall, not in the least bit boring. In an artistic or cultural environment where it's increasingly difficult to be original, a true original, this story does not disappoint. Shooting a mother and child delivers the goods—and leaving her wounded to die in the street, I think that's the cherry on the top. That's outrageous, if I'm not mistaken. It's definitely the kind of high note on which one could end a chapter. It will make people sit up and take notice.

Life, at times, may be stranger than fiction, but war is always stranger, there's no doubt about that, none at all. And it's something I've now experienced. As publishers, writing teachers, and all the other bombastic know-alls always say, write from experience. There will surely be a place for such a scene in my book—possibly the climactic moment—so I'll file it away with everything else for future use. One day I'm quite likely to be up on stage at some literary festival, trying to describe to my army of fans what it's like to shoot a mother and child. "But didn't you *feel* anything?" some middle-aged, grey-haired maid from suburbia will protest, indignant, nervously hovering on the outer edge of my spotlight. "How could you have done such a thing, Mr. Zorec? That's what I don't understand, how you can live with yourself." Everyone else in the auditorium will either applaud her or hiss to show their support for me, but none of them will remain silent, that's for sure. It'll be good for sales, such a story, because it will make me notorious.

Being a sniper—and this is the crux of the matter—being a sniper is an excellent way to define myself as a published author. Everyone understands that the public needs its writers to have a signature, a definition to which they can cling; one that explains, if only on a superficial, almost meaningless level, the person whose book they are purchasing. "Ah, look," a reader will say to his partner as they wander along the rows of shelves in the local bookshop, "Here's a new novel by Milan Zorec. He's that sniper fellow. Remember, the one who once shot a mother and child?" And he'll buy it, out of curiosity.

I ask myself if I've collected enough material. Do I have sufficient *ammunition* to create this never-before-seen novel? I've already filled one of my blue, A5 Collins 384-page notebooks—the ones I've always used for note taking—and am now on my second. I think there's a lot of good stuff in here, some great stories that could form the basis of an interesting novel. (Like a few days ago, this man walked out of a building down in the city holding a pistol to his head, shouting, looking up at the hills, and a minute later blew his own brains out. He saved us doing it for him. How considerate is that!) And if it doesn't make a great novel, or if I can't be bothered to write such a novel, then I could sell the notebooks themselves. Last November Bill Gates paid over thirty million dollars for a Leonardo da Vinci notebook, and that's definitely set me thinking. I mean, I can't help wondering, just briefly, if I could interest the computer nerd in purchasing—no, investing in—one of my notebooks, possibly both. I'd be happy enough with a million, in fact I'd be happy with any sum at all so long as it's greater than £500,000. As the kids in the school playground would have put it, in their crude, juvenile way, raising a rigid digit, "Spin on that, Mr. Information Man."

I have to admit I'm becoming increasingly preoccupied with sniping, and increasingly *less* preoccupied with my writing. Just conceivably, the creativity and artistry of my work in Sarajevo is proving to be more satisfying. It's certainly more financially rewarding than writing fiction. Soon I could even have enough money to visit Amis's dentist in the States. Gilhooley, who's been my partner for a few months now, has started to hint in a blatantly obvious, even mercenary way, that he deserves a percentage of my earnings. He even named a figure: forty percent of everything I earn, but I suspect that could be a bargaining ploy, an opening gambit. Needless to say, I'm not happy about this. I point out to him that although, financially speaking, my bottom line is extremely healthy (I never forget I'm addressing a headmaster), as yet I'm nowhere near as well off, say, as—picking a name at random—Mr. Martin Amis. So he'll definitely have to wait for any possible remuneration for his services. "Anyway," I add, "I always understood you were a volunteer?" He doesn't answer me.

The days have become hot and dry, a far cry from the snow and freezing temperatures when I arrived. Down near the city, on the outskirts, among the bombed-out remnants of the once-fine buildings, there's only dust and the stench of rotting corpses, which sometimes blow my way. Dogs wander wolf-like through the heat haze, all skin and bone, teeth bared in ghastly perpetual grins, yet with a bounce in their step, a cocky confidence that says they're celebrating the fact they've survived another winter—or is it simply another day?

The dogs are often the only sign of life, apart from the small number of people forced by hunger and thirst to leave their hideouts and go to one of the few shops still open for business, or to a well. There are the no-go areas of the city, full of lifeless buildings and empty streets. Rafters, charred and split, stick into the air like the ribs of a skeleton. Rubble lies in piles everywhere. Abandoned cars, riddled with bullet holes, most dismantled, rust on every corner. As I write, black smoke is billowing from a tall building near the Catholic cathedral, tonguelike flames licking the floors about halfway up, on the left-hand side. Yet in the streets that are hidden from the hills, it almost feels as though life's returning to normal again. A few trams are now running, and the UN presence is becoming more noticeable, with tanks and armored vehicles on many corners. I've also heard that more supplies are being carried into the city through the airport tunnel.

Once the city was very beautiful, with graceful Moorish and Ottoman-style buildings, and minarets rising above the tiled roofs of the old town. Now it is dead and scarcely worth fighting for.

It's the beginning of August, and word is coming in of Serbs being massacred in the Krajina region. Around two or three hundred thousand have been driven out by the

Croatian and Bosnian armies. Many have been killed and thousands displaced. To me it sounds like tit for tat "ethnic cleansing."

Milosevic is now making a show of washing his hands of the Bosnian and Croatian Serbs—my friends—because he can't persuade them to move to the peace table. Increasingly, he's retreating from his former position and making noises about wanting to settle the conflict. Meantime, morale among the Serbs in both Bosnia and Croatia, certainly among those in the camp, is going rapidly downhill and leadership is almost nonexistent.

Everyone around me is very worked up and swearing bloody vengeance for the Krajina attacks. It strikes me that they are acting—their posturings, mouthed obscenities, and displays of indignation and hurt are put on—with the sole intention of encouraging themselves to continue the battle. It also strikes me how greatly life has deteriorated in the six months since I arrived here. It's become a snuff movie. There's no one who can be relied on. Every single person is utterly alone. Clutching my rifle in the night, I've taken to slinking among the trees of the forest or crawling through the ruins of deserted buildings, on the prowl for prey. It's back to basics now. I am to kill or be killed; active or passive, victor or victim.

There's none of your Martin Amis flowery prose here. Plain words, the kind Sir Ernest Gowers would appreciate, are the order of the day. This is what it must have been like for Neanderthal man. I try not to think too much about whether I like this, because thinking is a part of my old life. It has no part in my life now. Possibly I should give up this journal for that very reason. I've moved beyond writing, now I only have time for living. Writing is the refuge of the weak, those who are too scared to take up the sword. Writing is dead. Maybe in the beginning was the Word, but it is not there now, not at the end. And the end, as the sandwich man in Oxford Street is always reminding us, is nigh.

I wonder if Amis believes writing is still relevant, if it has a place in the scheme of things. I suspect, for those who have attained his heights, any sense of artistic futility gives way to a sense of purpose when faced with the smothering comforts of success, when the reams of printed paper are drowned in scads of crisp banknotes. Those authors should come out here and see how long their scribblings keep them alive, whether they could hold at bay, with their pen nibs, the crowds screaming for their blood. Would they possess enough dictionaries and thesauruses to barricade themselves against the bullets, enough blotting paper to stem the tides of blood, enough word skills to kill those intent on putting the full stop at the end of their imaginative existences?

They (and I'm not sure I know who *they* are at this moment in time) talk about the adventure of language, but why, I ask myself, is it an adventure? Is it because one has to discover, put two and two together, experiment, try new phrases, new words—new worlds—work out what can be achieved with this flood of letters in one's head? So perhaps I haven't been adventurous enough. Perhaps I've been sticking too rigidly to the well-trodden paths, never venturing forth into the thickets of words on either side, never trusting myself to go where no man has been before. Did I lack the courage to go to those still unexplored regions, places that language hasn't yet reached?

I think I can now admit that *The Information* makes me feel a little like Salieri confronted by Mozart. The shamelessly extravagant wordplay casts a shadow over me that forces me to stumble around in the gloom, fossicking among the half-chewed words, the crumbs of phrases, the carelessly discarded sentences that fall from the Amis table. But then

I wonder if I'm even a Salieri. He definitely had some talent, and he's still talked about and played. He's survived two hundred years, if only as the joker in the Mozart pack. On the other hand, no one's ever compared me to Amis. No one's ever said, "Milan Zorec, now he has talent. If only he hadn't had the misfortune of being born at the same time as Martin Amis." I used to believe I hated Martin Amis—and all the others: Barnes, McEwan, Banville, Rushdie, Carey, Updike, Atwood, Proulx, DeLillo—but of course it isn't true. I admire them too much for that. I love them too much to hate them.

But what if I saw Amis walking through the streets below, would I be tempted to reach for my rifle? Of course I would, without any hesitation whatsoever. And for exactly the same reason that Salieri, as some would have it, poisoned Mozart. So that he, and all the other artists in the world, would no longer be reduced to a state of utter worthlessness. While Mozart was alive, Salieri's attempts at art were shown up as puerile and shallow, even meaningless. Without Mozart in the world, Salieri and all the others could flourish. If he didn't poison his friend, he certainly desired to do so in order to further the cause of art. And that's how I feel about Amis. At the moment he takes up too much space, he's too in my face.

We're rivals still, but now in different fields. Like him, I am an artist. Unlike him, I am an artist of ballistics. Balletic ballistics. The bullet possesses a fluency that Amis—and the rest—would envy. Each shot is beautifully composed: the speed of the small, golden missile, the friction as it rides the elements—wind, air, or rain—and the curve of its trajectory can be summed up in a mathematical equation.

My .308 Winchester round will travel one thousand yards in a fraction under two seconds. If I aim about ten feet above the target, the bullet will form a beautiful parabola, rising and falling as it spins through the ether and breaking the sound barrier as it does so, before hitting flesh. There, inside a human being, it will tumble head over heels through the skin, organs, and bones of the astonished person I have targeted. There is beauty in such destruction, and perfection, the beauty and perfection of figures, of a formula. The distance times the speed, with plusses and minuses to allow for the elements, divided by whatever, multiplied by something else . . . Take away the number you first thought of . . . And it would equal . . . What would it equal? Death? And if death, then hidden there among those figures is the formula for Life—Life with a capital L, the answer. And isn't that what every artist seeks? *Quod erat demonstrandum*, I am an artist. Of course, it's a slight problem that I know neither the right equation nor the right formula, but that's only a minor hiccup, a matter of time, of a little more research. The thing is, sniping has a precision no novelist will ever possess. It is a message, a communication without equivocation, it is information without risk of being misinterpreted. It is totally objective, absolutely finite. Sniping is everything that writing is not.

The author's fighting a losing battle. He sends his writing out into the world and has no idea where it'll end up, nor who'll pick it up. He doesn't even know if he has an audience "out there." He then has to hope that whatever he's written will be understood, that his message will be correctly interpreted. Writing is an inexact science, a shot in the dark without night-vision goggles. More than that, the gratification, if there is ever to be any, is delayed, possibly for years, sometimes for decades. It's anorgasmia for authors.

Words, like bullets out of gun barrels, spray across every corner of the globe every day of the year, unceasingly. But unlike bullets, most of those words miss their targets. Bullets are more likely to convey the feelings of the person holding the gun than words are to convey the feelings of the author holding the pen. The marksman communicates his thoughts more effectively than any writer, artist, or composer can. And you simply cannot argue with that. If you argue with that, I'll shoot you.

I have an audience, an audience that's part of my performance. These fellow performers, those on the receiving end of my communication, play an important part, which must not be underestimated or go unrecognized. They understand the missive that's been sent to them without equivocation. There's no need for them to puzzle over this message or wonder if they've understood what's being said. Their choice is then simple: to choose to die with grace, artistically, or, if my shot is imperfect, they can choose to put on a poor, less laudable performance. Yet even those hit less than perfectly can still perform well. Their swan song can be elegant, the steps they take can be beautiful, their gestures noble. When they crash to the pavement, it can be carried out with aplomb, the splattering of their brains on the ground can be done with all the artistry of Jackson Pollock.

There's no getting away from it, there's something grand about my achievements. It's not a book that I write with my rifle, but an opus. It's death on a grand scale, a magnum opus. Evil, some might say, although I can't see that myself, but if it's so then it's evil that has become a Magnificat. I'm not talking about petty stuff here. Not the cheating of the taxman of a few quid, not *borrowing* stationery from one's employer, not riding on the underground without a ticket, not pinching a magazine from the local newsagent. Nothing banal or everyday. No, here we are talking Dante and Milton, we are talking Lucifer, hell, and damnation. We are talking hideous evil, the stink of burning flesh, the bursting of boiling eyeballs, the screams of souls suffering indescribable torments, and so on and so on and so on.

I've exchanged—or am about to exchange—my pen for a rifle. This is an adventure proper, a real-life adventure, not something lived in the head. I'm in a country where words have no place, and I'll soon depart for another country where words have no place. Where the only language is written in blood, where one human being communicates with another by means of bullets, where the information is only received at death's door. It's where the mental becomes physical, where there's no place for wishy-washy scribes, where the scratchings of the nib give way to the crack of bullets and the splintering of bones. "Death," wrote Auden, "is like the rumble of distant thunder at a picnic." That is poetic. But, for me, it's too distant, too removed, too separate. Death for me is the splashing of someone's guts or brains in my face. It's as close as that.

I am trigger-*happy*. I am so trigger-happy I have to laugh.

There's now a lot of talk about us leaving the city. For the first time people are openly saying we won't be able to capture Sarajevo because the UN, after three years of doing little more than look on from the sidelines, is now becoming actively involved in the fighting. The Serbs are disappointed. After the longest siege in history, they don't have a lot to show for their efforts. The original idea was to win half of the city and then split it, like Jerusalem. We'd have one half and they'd have the other. Then someone decided we should try to win the whole city, if only because its occupants had proved so intractable and tenacious. That would be their reward for refusing to surrender—nothing at all. It now looks as though we'll be the ones who end up with nothing—apart from me. I'll have a story—my story.

I think back to a time in the playground, during a midday break, when I was having a cigarette and watching some kids, three boys of about nine or ten, surround this fat kid. He was hugging an article of clothing to his chest, a T-shirt or jacket, I couldn't really see, while he tried to turn his back on his tormentors. There were snot and tears all over his face, and even from where I was standing I could hear his squeaky, sniveling voice protesting. They were punching him, shoving him, attempting to yank the article of clothing from his grasp. It went on a long time, and I stood and watched them and wondered who'd win. I had a little bet with myself, but I got it wrong: the fat kid with the clothing won. He hung in there, gripping the jacket as if his very life depended on it, all the time being pummeled and kicked by the other three kids, until, finally, they gave up in disgust and walked away. Those people down there in the city, they're the same as that fat kid: they refuse to give up and now, disgusted and exhausted, we're about to walk off and let them keep their stupid city. We've had enough, we're bored. Maybe we'll find someone else we can pick on.

I'm trying to work out where I could go next. I have to go soon, somewhere, otherwise I'll end up staying here forever, or until this war ends—whichever comes first. I've had enough of the Balkans and this siege, this pantomime. Some of the men have been talking about moving on to Africa, to Zaire to fight for Mobutu, and others Kosovo, to fight against the Albanians. They're mercenaries, from all over, and they travel around to wherever there's a war. They're free, absolutely free, and I like that. They're paid well for what they do, too. Maybe I should go with them to Africa. They've told me they can help me arrange the paperwork. They say it's easy enough to do. I'm seriously thinking about it. Follow in the steps of Rimbaud, and give up art completely. But continue as a sniper, continue killing. Unlike Rimbaud, who only had it in him to do a spot of gun running—the limp-wristed pansy.

After spending only one night in the Vraca camp, I head for the forest northeast of the old military fortress that's situated on a hill above the old town. To the west I can see Kosovo Stadium and Olympic Hall, to the east is the road to Belgrade, and, less than twenty miles away, Mladic's bunker at Han Pijesak.

I've been spending more time away from camp, preferring the solitude of the hills to the moaning patriotism of the camp. I need this time by myself. I need the time to think and hatch my plot. My tent is pitched deep in the forest and well camouflaged. My only companion is a corpse in a copse a couple of hundred yards away. He looks—and stinks—as if he's been there for several weeks. As is common in this war, his face has been cut away to prevent recognition or, possibly, the imparting of *information*. He isn't going to be telling anyone anything, that's for sure. I don't suppose we knew each other anyway, even though I say hello and ask him how his day has been. He doesn't bother to reply, which I think is very rude. What's left of him is alive with maggots and flies and everything else in the forest that fancies a free feed.

At night the bombardments are spectacular. Mr. Gilhooley and I will sometimes watch them together. They remind us of fireworks in Hyde Park. The missiles fizz as they fly overhead the darkened city, some glowing white, like the milky secretions of a celestial snail, arcing through the blackness. Sometimes the night is lit up by pink tracer or antiaircraft fire. It's as if the city's besieged and their besiegers communicate by means of weaponry. The hissing of bullets, whistling of shells, fizzing of missiles, the crackling, booms, reports, thuds, and hammerings are the various ways in which they talk to each other. And at times they can be quite eloquent.

Beside me, Mr. Gilhooley oohs and aahs as he stares out at the man-made shooting stars in the night. It's quite an education for the headmaster. I tell him what a reversal of roles this must be for him, a headmaster being asked to keep lookout, like some small boy at the door of a classroom, to shout "Cave!" if anyone should appear. I receive the usual disdainful, superior grunt in reply, as if he's unable to demean himself by talking to me, the school janitor.

I stay away from camp for several nights. I want to be alone, and am alone—apart from Mr. Stinky just a short distance away. Finally I decide what I'll do.

I didn't go there immediately. It was not until a few weeks later, around mid-February, that I decided to pay them a visit. Their office was in Soho—no surprise there, I thought; how unoriginal. I went down an alley, past a Chinese restaurant. Inside there were people still having lunch, even though it was after three o'clock. The stink of rotting food filled the street. The pavements were dirty, almost greasy, making me wonder if the restaurant's kitchens had overflowed the premises. Cars were parked with two wheels on the curb, like dogs cocked against a fence. A line of open, uninviting doorways listed their residents on columns of small printed rectangular cards next to bell buttons. Some of the name cards were lit up. They were in number thirty-six.

I climbed the narrow stairs, telling myself to remain calm. I wasn't calm. My hands were forming fists, closing then opening spasmodically, and my jaw was clenched. All the way in on the underground I'd been talking to myself, muttering like some itinerant imbecile, unable to stop myself. It wouldn't do me any good to lose my temper, to rage—even though it might make me feel good. I stopped halfway up the stairs and concentrated on my heart rate, trying to slow it down. I had to be reasonable, but also firm and incisive. I had to explain why I'd come to visit them and point out how rude they'd been. Whatever happened, I must keep control of the heavy feeling of anger and resentment I was aware of within me, and had been aware of for days. I had every right to be angry, every right, but that didn't mean it would be wise to express it. I continued up the stairs. It was absurd: why did I have to beg such people to see me? Why did I have to go round on bended knee, cap in hand? By rights they should be begging to see me. It struck me that I was being unreasonably reasonable.

They were on the second floor, behind a frosted-glass door, sharing a corridor with three or four other small companies. A young woman, in fact a girl, looked up from behind what appeared to be an old pine kitchen table. She was in the process of shoving a manuscript into an A4 envelope: that was the first thing I noticed. A rejection, I thought, another rejection, and felt a momentary pang for the author— or would-be author. He or she was in the same boat as me. We were united against a common enemy. The girl smiled in a fake kind of way and asked if she could help me.

The reception was small and cramped. It was surrounded by walls and partitions, giving the impression that the offices behind were crowding in on the area, trying to squeeze it and push it out into the corridor. Apart from the receptionist's old kitchen table, there was a sofa, a coffee table with one of the day's newspapers on it, and a large empty vase on the floor in a corner. On one wall there were framed photographs of people I presumed were represented by the company. I didn't recognize any of them, although one could possibly have been Somerset Maugham. I wondered if all their authors were dead. The place felt more like a home than an office, and I supposed that was intentional: a desperate ploy to hide the fact that Mammon was involved.

Money, darling? Far too vulgar.

"I've come to see Mr. Mulqueeny," I said to the girl. I stood directly in front of the table and she looked me up and down quickly, as if she didn't want to be caught doing so. Her eyes flickered to a halt for a split second on the manila envelope I was holding to my chest. I knew she'd realize it was a manuscript, even though she didn't look particularly bright. She had doubtless seen more desperate would-be authors than I'd had cooked breakfasts, and had probably been trained to smell manuscripts from half-a-mile away. Like one of those dogs at airports—I half expected her to come and sit at my feet and stare at me until her handler arrived. It was possible she was the company's reader; she certainly looked stupid enough. When she'd finished looking me up and down in this disdainful way—it took all of two seconds—she asked, "Have you an appointment?" She knew I didn't.

"No." I couldn't be bothered to give her an explanation.

"I'm afraid Mr. Mulqueeny can't see anyone without an appointment. If you want to phone in sometime and make one . . ." Her voice trailed off. She obviously thought I was dumb, incapable of working out for myself what she was reluctant to say to my face: "No, Mr. Mulqueeny won't see you, and you can't make an appointment to see him." I knew she wouldn't have any trouble saying that over the phone. Many people find it easier to be rude over the phone.

"It's important I see him now."

"Well, I'm sorry, but . . ."

I was ready for this, in fact I expected it. I wasn't in the least surprised. If the girl had said, "Certainly, sir, Mr. Mulqueeny will be happy to see you now," I wouldn't have known what to do, I'd have been completely taken aback. But rejections, those I was used to, those I could deal with. I'd been the recipient of rejections all my life. I had a filing cabinet full of them. It was a hobby of mine, collecting rejections. I could have been a stand-in for Richard Tull in *The Information*.

"I'll wait." I turned away and went to sit on the sofa. "Will you tell him I'm here, so that I can see him when he's free? It won't take long." I smiled pleasantly, making an effort to hide my true feelings.

She stared at me. I think she was dumbfounded. (It's an interesting word, that. Like saying she had *found* a *dumb* way to look. "Flummoxed" might have been a more apt word. What's the difference between flummoxed and dumbfounded?

I wish I'd brought a dictionary to Sarajevo to help me with those kinds of question.)

"You can't just sit here, you know . . ." I noticed that her statements were all unfinished; she was a lover of ellipses.

I smiled at her, still pretending to be pleasant. She had long black hair. It was shiny, and looked very strokable. I'd like to have run my fingers through it. "Are you very busy at the moment?" I frowned, putting my head a little to one side as if I were genuinely interested and couldn't wait to hear her reply. I'm good at that, pretending to be interested in what someone is saying even though I'm not. I can fool the best of them.

She put down the envelope she'd been holding. I could see she was flustered, but then she can only have been about twenty, so that wasn't so surprising. Twenty-year-olds are easily flustered.

"Mr. Mulqueeny isn't here, you know, so he can't see you. And anyway," she added, in an attempt to strengthen her argument, "he's too busy to see anyone who just walks in off the street." She made me sound like a tramp. It was probably intentional.

"As I said, I'm happy to wait until he gets back. I haven't a lot on at the moment." I didn't believe her. Mr. Mulqueeny was probably right behind one of these walls, listening, his ear to the plaster, encouraging his employee telepathically. I picked up the newspaper on the table. The headlines were about the huge fees paid to the management of the new power companies, Power-Gen and National Power. I can't remember how much, just that I was disgusted by the string of noughts that seemed to fill all of one column—noughts that added up, not to nothing, but to a very substantial amount. I was assailed by that sense of déjà vu I always get when I open a newspaper. I didn't want to read about greedy, grasping businessmen, or Chechnya, or the Tories squabbling about Europe—or anything else, for that matter. I'd read it all before, far too many times. All that information, forests of it every day, and conveying precisely nothing. It was an assault on my brain, a perpetual bombardment of useless information that enlightened me not at all, and was simply intended to make me feel I was living in a democracy and much better off than the rest of the world. The only use for the tabloid rubbish I held in my hands was that it was a prop. It gave me something to do. I wanted to appear relaxed in front of the receptionist, if only because she was so young.

She disappeared through a door at the end of the room. That's promising, I thought. With any luck she'd gone to consult with Mr. Mulqueeny. See, it pays to stick your neck out in this game. People like this young girl need to be treated firmly, otherwise they think they can get away with their appalling behavior. I could hear the faint sound of voices in another room: it was the receptionist and someone else, someone who spoke very little, who was probably intent on listening to her rapid explanation of what had been happening in reception. It was a man though, I could tell that, and that was another good sign.

A minute later the girl came back into the room with a young man in tow. I cursed under my breath: another junior, certainly not Mr. Mulqueeny. He had the air of a novice and—although he was doubtless born on the right side of the tracks, probably dabbling in the arts until something better came along—he had a severe case of acne across his forehead. The receptionist veered away, like an escorting battleship from a destroyer about to engage the enemy, and went to watch from the safety of her table. I imagined commands being shouted, barrels being raised and lowered, loud whirrings and creakings as turrets swiveled, a frantic measuring of distance and speed as the young man closed in on me.

Then came the first broadside. It was a little cautious, an immature opening, more like a tentative feeler from a fencer than a naval broadside. "I'm afraid Mr. Mulqueeny hasn't been in the office today, can I possibly help?" He must have been in his mid-twenties, but already had a stooped and bookish air about him. He wore glasses and a grey, conservatively cut suit. I could feel his nervousness. His hands, which were probably damp, were clasping and unclasping themselves in front of his stomach, and his eyes were so watery he looked as if he were about to cry. I guessed he had an arts degree from Oxford or Cambridge, and it hadn't prepared him for this kind of thing.

"Are you expecting him? I'm happy to wait."

"Maybe I can help. I am Mr. Mulqueeny's assistant. Would it be about a manuscript?"

What else would it be fucking be about? That's what I thought, but I said, "Yes, it is. You're very perceptive."

He gave a polite, dismissive chuckle, as if he were too well brought up to be able to admit to the truth of what I'd said. "If you'd like to leave it with me, we'll be happy to look at it and get back to you."

I was impressed. He didn't even ask for a stamped, self-addressed envelope so that it could be returned to me posthaste. Because it would be returned, there was no question about that. It would be rejected immediately, we both knew that.

"You've already looked at it," and I gave him a big smile as if to reassure him that I didn't blame him personally for this unfortunate state of affairs. But it only succeeded in making him more flustered. He blushed, and the sweat stood out on his forehead. It must be embarrassing to be confronted by one of the firm's rejects.

"Oh, I see . . ." Another one who didn't like to complete his sentences, I thought. "I'm sorry to hear that, but don't despair. You may well have better luck with another literary agent. Have you tried another literary agent? I could suggest some names, if you'd like. Would you like some names? Let me get them for you." Instead of engaging with the enemy as he originally intended, he was now frantically trying to disengage.

I'm sure you could suggest some names. Anything to get rid of me, pass the buck on to someone else, and let them do the dirty work. The receptionist was pretending to busy herself behind her table, but I could see she was watching us from beneath lowered brows.

"I want to ask Mr. Mulqueeny why he rejected my man-uscript," I said to the young man's half-turned back as he set off to look for some names. There, it was out. I was quite calm and collected. I was proud of myself.

It was the young man who was increasingly losing it. "But you understand, Mr. . . . ?" he said, turning back to me.

I gave him my name. Why not help the lad out?

"But I'm sure you understand, Milan," (this is a little familiar, I thought) "we're unable to offer individual criti-cism on every manuscript we receive. It simply isn't feasible, as much as we'd like to." He waved his arms feebly toward the door through which he'd made his entrance with the receptionist. "You should see my office. Manuscripts piled . . ." Another sentence petered out between us. How high are the manuscripts piled, I wondered: as high as his desk, the ceiling, this building, an elephant's eye, I had no idea. He didn't elaborate on the height of the manuscripts, but con-tinued to explain his predicament to me in breathless bursts. "Even if we wanted to . . . You have no idea the number . . . If you had read our rejection letter . . . It's all there . . . We do the best we can, but of course . . ." Unfinished sentence followed unfinished sentence in a staccato of explanations. I tried mentally to catch some of them as they flew past my ears. His hands, as though exhausted by their owner's verbal excesses, flopped to his sides, and he stopped talking, like a windup toy whose battery had run out. He looked at me, possibly hoping I might come to his assistance. The receptionist had pushed him into the frontline, and he wasn't having much success. Having fired all his guns, he now wished to retreat back into the trenches.

"I'd like an individual criticism from Mr. Mulqueeny." I remained pleasant; after all, he was only a kid. But it wasn't easy to stay calm. I was beginning to imagine my hands around his neck, squeezing the carotid artery, staring into bulging, upturned eyes. "I'm happy to wait until he's free, as I said to the young lady over there." I returned to my newspaper, adding over the top of it, "I think I deserve that." The young man and the receptionist exchanged a look, as if to say, "What do we do now?"

They were rescued from their dilemma by the arrival of a middle-aged man, probably about ten years older than me, thickset, not tall, throwing open the front door and bursting into the office. He was all bustle and self-importance, I could see that straight away. He looked like someone who had inhaled deeply, but forgotten to exhale. He had glasses resting on the end of his nose, over which he peered at the three of us, a bald head—apart from a sparse arrangement of fine salt-and-pepper hair around the edges—and was wearing a rather shabby, loose-fitting, dark suit. He was clutching at least six manuscripts to his chest with one hand, and carrying a briefcase in the other. I had no doubt that this was the man himself. He'd been out of the office after all. Without saying good morning to his young employees, he dropped the manuscripts onto the table with a peremptory "Send these back, Diane," and turned to go through to his office. The young man leapt after his boss, determined not to let this life raft drift too far off. "Mr. Mulqueeny . . ."

They conferred together in whispers at the end of the room, the older man turning every so often to scowl at me across the top of his glasses. He said something to the young man, sighed loudly as if it were all too much, and disappeared through a door. The young man came toward me. "Mr. Mulqueeny has kindly agreed to see you for a few minutes. You're very lucky, this is most unusual."

I couldn't bring myself to thank him; I simply nodded. Was he expecting me to make obeisance with deep gratitude there and then? I wasn't sure. Five minutes later the receptionist took me through to Mr. Mulqueeny's office, introduced me, and left. He was sitting behind a desk, his baby face barely visible above the numerous piles of manuscripts that covered it. He neither got up from his chair nor held out a hand, obviously thinking that by agreeing to see me he'd already extended sufficient civility. I was waved toward a chair, the only one in the small room apart from his own. Even with the desk between us, I was assailed by fumes of alcohol and garlic. It had obviously been a good lunch— probably with some best-selling author, I thought.

The man with his name on the door didn't waste time on polite chitchat. He took a deep breath and started straight in. "What some of you people don't understand is that the book industry is exactly that: an industry. It's a business. It has profit and loss columns, a bottom line, earnings and dividends, and so on and so forth. It's about money, it's not about art. People come through these doors with airy-fairy dreams about art, immortality, and literature—you can put all of those with capital letters: Art, Immortality, and Literature. I'm not interested in those. I don't give a damn about any of that. Art, Immortality, and Literature will never be welcomed through these doors. You know what interests me?"

I shook my head. Not only did I not know what interested him, I had no idea why he was telling me all of this.

"How much money is in it for me, that's all that interests me. I don't give a twopenny-halfpenny damn if your novel is the greatest novel since *War and Peace* or if you're a better writer than Conrad, I want to know how much money your book is going to make for me. I want to know if it's going to help me pay off my mortgage, let my wife buy herself beautiful dresses—which she's extremely partial to—and allow me to fork out the ridiculous amounts of money I'm expected to pay for my children's education."

As he spoke, he was waving his arms around in the air as if addressing a far larger audience than one. "Now, my dear sir, if you can persuade me that you're the next Michael Crichton, Jean Auel, Stephen King, Danielle Steel—even the next Nick Hornby—then I shall welcome you with open arms. But I suspect you're more likely to be, at the very best, a one-shot wonder, the author of an autobiography masquerading as a novel, of little literary merit and no page-turning qualities, that will cost a publisher a lot of money to promote and cost me my reputation for having pushed it onto him." He burped quietly—"Excuse me."—before carrying on.

"It's true publishers pay first novelists a pittance, and I'll tell you why this is so. It's because it is more expensive for publishers to persuade the public to buy *your* novel than it is for them to pay an advance of thousands of pounds to a well-known and already well-established author. That's what people like you don't realize. Publishers don't pay novice novelists £5000 in the hope of getting £5000 back. They want more back. They are speculators, and as speculators they want profits. The fact of the matter is, around eighty percent of all published novels are failures. Eighty percent, and I'm talking all novels, not just first novels."

It was a tirade. He just went on and on. Beneath the bustling, vaguely literary intellectual there lurked the hard, cold businessman, and the latter was all that was visible to me. Exhausted, if not drowned by the oceans of words that had washed over him throughout his life, Mulqueeny had become indifferent to the struggles of would-be writers. He was impassive toward both me and my book, and my plight was of no interest to him. Eventually he stopped talking, and there was a long silence while he stared at me over his glasses.

"Mr. Mulqueeny, I believe I have talent. In fact I know I have talent."

"My dear sir, they all say that. Try to be more original." He yawned. "Anyway, you're too old. How old are you?"

"I'm thirty-six."

"They like authors to be in their twenties nowadays. Gives them more of a career."

I ignored him. "All I'm asking is for someone to tell me where I'm going wrong. I've written novels—the one I submitted to you was my fourth—and I've written short stories, many short stories. And they all come back with the standard rejection slip. No one tells me anything, no one offers me any kind of help or advice."

"That's because there are too many of you. There are millions of wannabe writers out there, millions. If I saw every person who asked for help, I wouldn't have time to do anything else. I'd have to shut up shop." He put his feet up on his desk, among the manuscripts, and stared briefly out of the window. Solely for my benefit, he was doing his impersonation of a bored man. But he didn't fool me. I could see that he was a pompous fool, and he was also beginning to irritate me.

"It's a vicious circle, that's what you're telling me. I won't have a novel accepted by a literary agent unless I've been published, and I won't be published until I've had a book accepted by a literary agent."

He raised his eyebrows. "That is very perspicacious of you."

"But how do you know I'm not the next Martin Amis? To pick a name at random."

"As I said, you're too old." He shrugged and gave me a quick, almost sympathetic smile, but lacking in sincerity. "He published his first novel when he was twenty-four."

"Only because of Daddy."

"You think so?"

"Of course. Doesn't everyone?"

"I wouldn't be so sure. His talent was recognizable, I think, even then."

"*The Rachel Papers* is juvenilia. If it had arrived on your desk with my name on the front cover, you'd have thrown it in the bin."

"That's your opinion."

"It's a fact. Anyway, I'm not yet thirty-seven and Annie Proulx was over fifty when her first novel was published. So was Saramago. I may not be an Oxford or Cambridge undergraduate, but I'm definitely not too old."

"Those two writers you mention, Proulx and Saramago, are geniuses. You, I am afraid, are not—whatever you might think. You know my advice to you? Give it up. Give up your dream of literary immortality or of writing a best-selling airport novel—whichever dream it is you have—and stick to your day job. Be content with being a waiter, plumber, schoolteacher, journalist, businessman, electrician, undertaker, dishwasher, or whatever it is you do, and forget about being a writer. You've missed the boat. If you'd wanted to be an author in the eighteenth century, in the days of Jane Austen say, you'd possibly have succeeded. Hardly anyone wanted to be a novelist then. Publishers were crying out for writers. Today every man and his dog wants to be a novelist."

"Fuck Jane Austen," I said, leaning forward in my chair.

"Certainly, but have you seen what she looked like?" He smiled, obviously amused by my outburst.

"I have talent."

"If you have talent, sir, if you really have talent, then you'll be published."

"But you rejected my manuscript."

"Then we obviously don't agree that you have talent, or not sufficient talent."

"Maybe you wouldn't recognize talent if it was shoved up your arse."

He raised his eyebrows and lowered his feet to the ground. He swiveled his chair round to face me. I now had his full attention.

"There is the possibility that I wouldn't recognize talent if it was, as you so charmingly put it, shoved up my arse, but I happen to believe that I would. However, in the unlikely event I didn't recognize it, then you can rest assured someone else would. It might take time, but if you truly have talent, someone out there will eventually realize it. Not necessarily immediately, but eventually."

"My book was good—*is* good. The plot is strong, the characters are rounded, the dialogue is excellent, the narrative is well written—it's good."

I was hoping he'd ask for a rundown of the plot, but he didn't, so I prompted him. "Let me remind you what it was about." I doubted he would remember it—or even have read it.

"I'm too busy for that."

"It won't take long." And I started to give him the plot of my rejected novel. After only speaking for a minute or two, I could see he was becoming more and more fidgety. Suddenly he stood up. "I haven't the time for this. I have too much work to do. I'm sorry, but you'll have to leave. Possibly another day."

I too stood up. I went around his desk. He stepped back, stumbling against his chair. I pushed him into it, and it rolled a little over the floor until it came to a stop against a pile of manuscripts. I bent over him, placing my hands on the arms of his executive chair. It squeaked. If I'd been a vampire I would have been repelled by the waves of garlic that hit me full in the face. Mr. Mulqueeny looked alarmed. At the risk of sounding like an airport novel . . . *My eyes bored into his. Steely eyes, ice-cold resolve. A vein on the side of my forehead throbbed menacingly. I was determined to get my own way, come hell or high water.* That kind of thing.

"Are you sitting comfortably?" I asked, speaking slowly, emphatically. "Then I shall continue with my story. Thank you." I straightened up, walked back around the desk, sat down, and continued to recount the plot of my novel.

But I'd lost the thread of what I'd been saying. I found it hard to concentrate. I was too aware of Mulqueeny fidgeting, forever looking at the phone on his desk as if he might find the courage to spring up and grab it. I stopped my sales spiel. He was making me angry.

"You're not listening, Mr. Mulqueeny."

"I am, truly I am." He was nervous.

"Who read my novel at Mulqueeny & Holland? Who read the first three chapters and the synopsis? That receptionist out there? You?"

"No, not me. I don't read novels." He said it too quickly.

"You brought a pile of manuscripts into the office this morning. I imagine they were novels?"

"Yes, that's true, but it's most unusual. I normally leave the novels to my readers. We have three or four readers and we go by what they say, by their recommendations."

"But you could have read my manuscript. You, yourself. It's possible. Do you recognize the plot?"

"I can't say that I do."

"You can't say that you do?" I almost whispered it.

"You see, we read so many, so very many manuscripts, it can be difficult to remember them all. Keeping track of everything . . . You don't understand . . ."

"But you only read the first page. It can't be that difficult to remember one page." I started to take my manuscript out of the envelope. "I'll read you the first page. It may jog your memory."

He half laughed, holding up a hand. "We do usually read a bit more than that. It can be hard to judge a book from the first page, you know."

"It must be hard to judge a book from the first three chapters and a synopsis, I'd have thought, but you manage that all right."

"You obviously don't appreciate the size of our task. Another lifetime would not be long enough. Publishers and literary agents are being crushed by the sheer weight of submitted manuscripts. We receive over three thousand a year. We cannot give careful consideration to every single novel that comes into our offices—as much as we'd like to. It's an impossibility."

"My problem is I don't give a fuck about anyone else's novel, I'm only interested in mine."

"I understand. But try to see it from our point of view. The system's not ideal for us either. It's a gamble. We have to rely on gut instincts—a quick glance through a few pages, a snap judgement, and, if we get it wrong, we miss out on a best seller. It's easy for people like you to read a published novel at your leisure, to say, this is a book of great literary merit, but I challenge you to pick that same book out of the pile of manuscripts on your desk at the end of every day. When you're tired, when you're pushed for time, when all you want to do is go home, put your feet up, and have a glass of wine. When you've spent the whole day, every day of the week—let's face it—

wading through a pile of dross. Ninety-nine times out of a hundred, *dross.*"

"My heart goes out to you." I'd started to pace up and down his office while he spoke. We were going round in circles: I was letting him speak too much, and all he was coming up with was excuses. As for me, I was listening too much.

It happened quickly. I wasn't thinking, I just did it. There was a vase of flowers on a cabinet at the end of his desk. It was a tall vase; I thought the flowers were gladioli or something, but I wasn't sure. I pushed the top of the vase and it fell across the desk, pouring a considerable amount of water onto the publisher's lap. The effect was good. Water and flowers cascaded everywhere, including over a pile of manuscripts waiting to be rejected—or already rejected—on a corner of the desk. Mr. Mulqueeny stumbled to his feet, looking down at his wet crotch, his face a picture of horror. I think maybe it was then that he understood I was serious. His mouth opened. He was gasping for air, as if he might have been a fish emptied out of the flower vase. He tried to dry the front of his trousers with tissues from a box on his window sill.

"I'm interested in my novel, Mr. Mulqueeny. As I said to you before, other people's books are of no interest to me. I want you, or whoever read my book, to tell me why it was rejected. That's all. Why? That's all I wish to know. A simple enough question, I'd have thought. I want to know where, in your opinion, I went wrong. I want to know what, in your opinion, I'm doing wrong. I want to know why, in your opinion, my story lacks appeal. I want some guidance and advice. That's all I'm asking for. Not too much, surely? I don't wish to argue with you—you're entitled to your opinion—I simply want some help." And I pushed, with deliberate slowness, a pile of manuscripts resting near the edge of his desk onto the floor. Just to add insult to injury.

He stared at me, wide-eyed, his mouth still open, still gasping. He had one hand resting on his desk as if to prevent himself from falling over. "I'll tell you what . . ." He cleared his throat. "Excuse me. Let me just have a look at our files. We should be able to find out who read your manuscript, and we can ask them for a more detailed evaluation." He smiled in a sickly fashion. "How's that?"

"That sounds like an excellent idea."

"Please have a seat. I'll be right back."

He edged around me, giving me as wide a berth as possible in the small room—yet I still caught a noseful of alcohol fumes—and scuttled crabwise through the door.

Over his shoulder: "I'm sorry. Your name?"

"Zorec. Milan Zorec."

"Ah yes."

I sat down in my chair and gazed around me. I was pleased with myself, I was making progress. I was one up on all the other writers whose works lay scattered in various piles around the office.

Everything was quiet. Outside the window was the distant, perpetual drone of London traffic. A patch of dull grey sky was sewn onto the gap between the top of the window and the roof of the building opposite. Someone in the street below shouted, and I could hear the distinctive sound of a lorry reversing. I picked up the nearest manuscript. It was written by someone in Sussex—Horsham, I think. It was called *The Barking Cat*. I hated the title. The synopsis started off something like: "My book is about a bunch of New York Mafiosi who go with their wives and children for a holiday in London." It didn't sound too promising, but then anything that starts, "My book is about . . ." isn't going to sound promising. I didn't understand the significance of the title, nor the connection with the Mafiosi. I flicked to the first page. "Luigi pumped the London cabbie for his life

story, but hadn't reckoned on the famous British reserve."
I threw the manuscript back on its pile. I agreed with that
particular decision of Mr. Mulqueeny and his gang of readers: instant rejection. Too obvious. My book was much better than that.

The literary agent came back into the room. He still
looked very nervous. He had nothing in his hands. "Diane
is looking for your reader's report. Of course, you have to
appreciate the report is confidential. You understand we
can't give you the name of the person who read your book."

"Why not? I only want to talk to him."

"It's out of the question, I'm afraid. We have to pre-
serve our readers' anonymity."

"It's not that I want to argue with him or anything. I
simply want to hear where he thought I went wrong."

"I can tell you that, but I absolutely cannot give you a
name and address. Some of our would-be authors get quite
upset when their manuscripts are rejected."

"Is that right?"

He smiled faintly and his eyes flickered to the broken
vase on the floor.

A few minutes later there was a commotion in reception. A door banged, and there were voices. A few seconds
later the receptionist came tentatively into the office, followed closely by two policemen. Mr. Mulqueeny looked at
me quizzically, waiting to see my reaction, then gave a quick
smile and shrug as if to say, *What else could I have done—
you gave me no other option.* I should have realized. I stared at
the two policemen. I was angry with myself for not having
foreseen him acting in such an idiotic manner.

He rose to his feet. "This man is quite crazy. He threw
that vase at me—look at my trousers! And all over these
manuscripts. And now he's threatening me." He preened
himself, pleased to have survived what he perceived as his

ordeal, and yet I hadn't done half of what I'd imagined do-ing. The policemen asked me to accompany them down to the station. I shrugged. One of them even produced some handcuffs. I said they weren't necessary. He looked disap-pointed.

As we were leaving his office, Mr. Mulqueeny called out to me. I turned. "The person who read your book by the way—I think you should know—she said you had a medio-cre talent. She also said: 'I feel I've read this before.' Those were her exact words, Mr. Zorec—that your book was hard-ly original." Like a child who has reached the sanctuary of "home" and is intent on baiting his playmates, he grinned at me from behind his desk. I almost expected him to stick out his tongue and say "Nyah nyah ni nyah-nyah!" If the police hadn't been there I might have killed him at that moment. He was lucky.

When we walked through the reception area, the girl behind the desk, Diane, standing next to the young man, started to giggle. She had her hand up to her mouth. She was fucking laughing at me. I'd have killed her on the spot, too, if the police hadn't been there.

So I ended up in prison, in a police cell. I spent the night cooling my heels—now where does *that* expression come from? I had to share the cell with a drunk driver and a down-and-out (who stank). I was released in the morning because Mr. Mulqueeny didn't press charges: he'd simply wanted me removed from his office. I was cautioned not to go any-where near the literary agent's offices again. For a time I toyed with the idea of going back. I imagined what I'd do to them all. The Oxbridge graduate never featured greatly in these daydreams; I'd simply shoot him. Mr. Mulqueeny I'd tie to his chair while I fucked his receptionist, Ms. Diane, the one who'd laughed at me, on his desk in front of him, among all the rejected manuscripts. Then I'd kill the literary agent by stuffing manuscripts down his throat and up his backside and setting fire to them. They wouldn't have seen any of that before, oh no. In fact the only reason I didn't do any of this was because I suspected there was a strong likelihood of being caught, and I didn't want to spend years in prison for such worthless people. Especially not then, after the idea of going to Sarajevo came to me.

But for a while I dreamt of getting that receptionist back, of giving her a warm *reception*, of getting my revenge on Ms. Diane. I'd make sure she wasn't so quick to laugh at me in the future, that was for sure.

There's the definite feel of a finale about the scene, as if soon the curtain will fall and the audience—us up in the hills—will be able to go home. The war has reached its autumnal stage. It has grown into a tragedy, even though I've grown to regard it more and more as a comedy—of errors. The war is flawed, it's a lost cause, the siege has reached the point of terminal decline. I'm reminded of the final day of a school term, with everyone preparing to leave. The kids' minds (if kids can be said to possess such a thing) are elsewhere, the work has been pushed to one side.

Today, 29 August, I returned to the Vraca memorial park camp in the evening to be told that thirty-eight people had been killed in Sarajevo's main marketplace, the Makale. It's the same marketplace where sixty-nine people were killed in another mortar attack about eighteen months ago. The funny thing is, it's supposed to be a safe area. So much for the UN.

I gather we're blaming the enemy—and why not? That's how it's done nowadays: you commit an atrocity, then tell the world's media that the enemy killed themselves for the publicity, to try to win the sympathy vote. I've never understood this dodging of responsibility for one's actions; to me it doesn't make sense. If you commit an atrocity, why not admit to it? When that Pan Am jet was blown up over Lockerbie, everyone ran around denying they'd done it. But someone must have done it, and been proud to have done it, so what's the point in remaining silent? If you feel so strongly about a cause that you're willing to blow up a planeload of people, but refuse, once you have the world's undivided attention, to admit you did it, why place the bomb in the first place? The IRA always admits to its bombings, and I like that. "Yeah, sure enough, pal, it was us that did it. We put that bomb in the pub that killed eight people and maimed fourteen others, and we're more than happy to admit it." That kind of talk makes sense to me.

The rumor is that one of the batteries on the eastern side of the city lobbed the offending mortar into the marketplace. The question, if anyone can be bothered to either ask or answer it, is: were they ordered to fire at the innocent people out shopping, or did some bored artilleryman fire the shell into the marketplace to liven things up? For what it's worth, I think Mladic gave the order. He may even have fired the gun himself. It's pure Ratko, exactly the kind of thing he loves doing. Killing people is his forte, and a whole crowd of shoppers in a market would have had special appeal.

Around the campfire they were all talking about the marketplace slaughter. Something different had happened, and the men regarded it as a break from the usual routine. Like me, they were pointing out that Mladic always concentrates his guns on civilian targets. He's been doing it for the past three years, telling his soldiers to shoot only where there's flesh. What they do, in fact, is no different from what I and the other snipers do every day. It's all relative. No one objects if a team of snipers succeeds in killing thirty-eight people in a day, but when a mortar does the same thing, everyone gets upset. Can someone explain the difference to me? Once, when Mladic was visiting camp, I heard him say, "It's the quickest way to get them to surrender. Kill the ordinary people and it'll cause such an outcry it will make them give up the city. Anyway," he added, winking at one of his aides, "that's exactly what they are, *ordinary*, so what does it matter?" I don't understand why everyone feels the need to discuss this Makale thing endlessly. It's as if they're determined to justify their actions. I don't see any need for that. It doesn't worry me at all if there's little reason and no excuse for what I'm doing. Why should it? Mallory climbed Everest because it was there. I'm killing the inhabitants of this city for the same reason—because they're there.

Nikola, as usual, was disagreeing with everyone. "Just the day before the Makale bomb, that pig Richard Holbrooke said he'd bomb us to the negotiating table. That's what he said: 'I'll bomb the Serbs to the negotiating table.' So it's obvious enough he did this. He wants the world to hate us even more than they do already by making out we bombed those shoppers. One day he says that, and the very next day the market is shelled. And the following day US planes just happen to be ready to bomb us back to the Stone Age—to punish us. That's the word they used: to punish us. It's too much of a coincidence." The men who were listening to him wavered, like the crowd in *Julius Caesar*, many of them nodding and muttering that he could be right. The giant, Bukus, who'd wandered over to listen to the discussion, shook his head impatiently and shouted, "Fuck the lot of them, that's what I say. Who's coming up to the farmhouse?" And he strode off, obviously having more important things on his mind than politics.

Nikola blames the disaster on international public opinion. He says the UN, the US, the UK, and Europe, who have all stood by and done nothing over the past few years, have now said enough's enough. Those mealymouthed spectators are becoming impatient with the Serbs. There's been too much bloodshed, that's their opinion. It strikes me as a bit late for the appeasers, the Western powers, to get upset about the amount of blood that's been spilt. They've sat on their hands and been humiliated by Serbia for as long as I can remember, so why show concern now? Maybe they have a limit to the amount of blood they'll allow to be spilt. Like nine hundred gallons is OK, but one thousand gallons, that's too much. The bombing of the marketplace was a mistake—if we did it. We pushed them too far. There's been such an outcry about "the barbarians besieging the city" that the West now feels obliged to take action. They can no longer afford to keep their heads buried in the sand. The British, the Americans, and the Europeans are finally realizing that you can't remain uninvolved, can't negotiate, can't say, "Hey, let's sit down and chat about this," with people like Milosevic, Mladic, and Karadzic. Those three individuals are up to their elbows in blood and still busy, busy, busy killing their enemies and turning their backs on the peace conference.

That doesn't mean I'm not upset now that the UN has started to bomb us. Luckily, I'm not in Grbavica. It's bearing the brunt of the UN bombing runs. I've spent much of the day looking across the city as the jets streak overhead, holding my breath until, a few seconds later, there's an explosion and smoke erupts from within the huddle of buildings. They're bombing other positions around the city too, but less severely. I hope they don't hit the big farmhouse.

I wonder what Mladic and Radovan Karadzic will do. To start with, it might be a good idea if they talked together. It's being said they hate each other now, Mladic calling the president a corrupt war profiteer and refusing to talk to anyone but Milosevic. He's also promised, without consulting Karadzic, that if the UN bombs our positions around Sarajevo then he'll bomb London. Great, I think, fantastic! That would be interesting, although I can't see Milosevic agreeing to such a maneuver, even if they're capable of it. Mind you, if it did happen, I'd immediately write to Bridgette and tell her that the bombing raids had been arranged by me in the hope of wiping her off the face of the map, blowing her and her *creative* right out of their bed—the ultimate lover's revenge. She's so naive she'd probably believe me. And then, of course, there's also Ms. Diane . . .

One thing for sure is that the beast of war is out there, loose in the land. I can feel it. There's blackness everywhere, the rumbling of God knows what, like something out of Conrad: anarchy, the breakdown of the rule of law, men roaming the land slaughtering each other among smoking ruins. *The horror, the horror!*

I recall Santo, many months ago, muttering something about how we all believe we're good until a war starts, but it's only when it does that we truly find out who we are, only then that we know for certain whether we're good or bad.

"There's a wild beast in all of us, Milan," he said, half turning to rest a hand on my shoulder, as if to make sure I didn't escape the truth he was about to reveal, "and most of us are only too happy to let it out if we do not have to answer for its actions."

When the barriers come down, that's what he was saying, when the restrictions, rules and laws are removed, when we have no one to answer to but ourselves, that's the time when we find out the kind of person we are.

Me, I think I'm bad. It's not necessarily some amazing insight, but I think that's the kind of person I am—bad. And now's the time to prove it to myself.

Yesterday morning, without telling anyone, I returned to my place in the forest, back with my neighbor, Mr. Stinky. And that evening I made my move. I left a few things in the tent I knew I wouldn't need—among them my notebooks and *The Information*. I put enough food for one night into my rucksack, and headed back to Grbavica, to the less busy, easterly edge of the suburb. I moved into an apartment on the sixth floor of a block. It meant I could see farther, but also that I was farther from my targets, not that I was too concerned by that.

Today, a little before noon, I started downstairs. I moved in a dream, my mind quite blank, as if hypnotized. I carried only my rifle. Because the stairs were at the back of the building, facing toward the mountains, I was out of sight of any enemy snipers in the city. At the foot of the stairwell I paused. No one was to be seen. I edged along the outside of the apartment block and stopped at the corner. About fifty yards away, on a slight elevation, was a bungalow. It must have been quite grand once upon a time, with its extensive gardens and small driveway, but the surrounding walls were now mostly destroyed, and the garden was bare of everything except weeds. Between myself and the house was open, rough ground that offered virtually no cover. To my right was a minor road that ran around the lower slopes of Mount Trebevic until it joined the main road to Pale. Scarcely anyone used it nowadays: for the locals it was too close to the front line, and for the besiegers there were better, less exposed roads that would take them in the same direction. There was little chance I'd be seen from this road. I crouched low and ran across the open ground, stopping only when I was directly behind the bungalow. I realized one of our snipers was inside, although I didn't know who. The building was low, the gaping window holes perfectly aligned with the city streets below. It was a great position for sniping. There was no sign of activity, but then one hardly expected to see or hear any signs of life coming from a sniper's aerie. I knew it would be unlikely for anyone inside to be looking out the back, unless he happened to be taking a break. A sniper wouldn't worry about any activity from that direction, that was for sure—his own side, his supposed friends, were behind him. The ground fell away before me, not steeply but gradually, to another apartment building, very similar to the one I'd just left, and my destination. I walked, almost casually, my rifle at my side. The road had veered away to the right, and I was out of sight of any snipers in the city. Momentarily, I relaxed. Once I was close to the rear of the apartments I became more cautious. From here I knew it was dangerous territory: reaching where I wanted to be meant exposing myself briefly on two sides. The main danger was from UN and Bosnian snipers in the city, who observed these buildings and the surrounding ground continually. There was also the man himself. If he recognized me I'd be safe, but if he mistook me for one of the enemy he'd kill me without a second thought. There was also possible danger from a third source: if the guns behind me, in the mountains, got their calibrations wrong and a shell fell short of the front line, it could land right on top of me. It had happened before. It wasn't likely, and there was nothing I could do about it anyway, so there was little point worrying.

I wanted to get to an area about a hundred yards diagonally in front of the block of apartments in which he was positioned. It was in a kind of no-man's-land down near the river. I knew the layout of the ground there: it was riddled with ruined outhouses, sheds, and bushes. Shell craters, mud, weeds, and rusting machinery lay in between. If I made it that far, there'd be plenty of cover, but it was reaching there that was the risk.

I was feeling very calm. I skirted around the back of the apartments, keeping some distance between myself and the building, and ducked behind a hedge. Bent double, I made my way to the end of the hedge, crouched down, and waited. Twenty yards away, across rough ground, was a wooden shed—or the remains of one. Only a few planks of wood still stood upright on each of its four sides. If it hadn't been situated in such a dangerous spot, it would have disappeared completely by now, used as firewood. I ran across to it. For a fleeting moment I wondered if this was worth the risk, and the possibility entered my head that I'd gone mad. My main worry, of course, was that he wouldn't be there. I knew it was his favorite sniping spot, but I also knew he moved around quite a bit rather than stay in the same place every day. That would risk drawing attention to himself.

When I'd caught my breath and studied the layout of the land ahead, I crept forward to a bush at the end of the wooden shed and then, keeping as low as possible, ran along behind the remains of an old stone wall. About a hundred yards past the apartment block, I headed to my left, directly toward the frontline. I picked out a ruined outhouse and a few bushes in front of me. This was the most dangerous part. I'd be a sitting duck if he didn't recognize me, and I'd be exposed to snipers in the city at the same time.

The sweat stood out on my forehead and ran down into my eyes. I was saturated, but as soon as I stopped moving I felt the chill on my skin. I considered turning around and going back, but thought it was too interesting an experience to pass up. I told myself not to be pathetic: this is what it's like to live down in the city, this is how exposed they must feel as they walk along the street. With that grim consideration in mind, I ran for the cover of the ruined outhouse.

Even when I reached it, I didn't feel safe. Now I was

certainly exposed to him. If he didn't immediately realize who I was . . .

Had he seen me? Was he even there? I turned cautiously, not hiding my face, even though I half expected a bullet to smash into it at any second. It was difficult not to screw up my eyes.

I was in the perfect spot, well hidden from any sniper in the city. I could be seen only from the apartment block then. It was less than a hundred and fifty yards away, possibly a hundred and thirty. I scanned the windows, most of them—if not all of them—without glass. The black rectangular holes dotted the face of the nondescript building, a few covered with plastic sheeting.

Then I saw an almost imperceptible movement on about the sixth floor, in a corner window. If I hadn't been looking for it, I wouldn't have noticed. I guessed it was the barrel of a rifle. I was being watched, I knew that, I could feel it; my senses were working overtime. I wanted to shut my eyes against the impact of a bullet, but instead forced myself to smile and wave. The tip of the barrel was lowered, raised again, as if for a second look through the telescopic sights, then lowered once more. The figure retreated from the window. I guessed what he was doing: he wanted to be in a position to see me, but remain out of sight of enemy snipers. He stood up. It was him. I recognized him from his body shape—stocky. I could see him clearly. It was him, no doubt at all. I'd guessed right: he was there. He was gesticulating, slapping his thighs, possibly laughing that machine-gun laugh of his: *huh, huh, huh, huh!* It was hard to tell. But I could imagine his baby face all lit up, his boyish enthusiasm. I scanned the other windows and could see no one else. I raised my rifle above my head and laughed out loud. I even did a little jig. He was signaling to me, doing his best to be friendly, trying to worm his way into my good books—my good books! That's a laugh, that's poetic. What would he know about good books?

I understood what he was saying from his gestures: "What are you doing here? What brings you to this god-forsaken spot?' That's how he would have put it, and those were the words Mulqueeny would have used too. "You can't just barge in here uninvited, you know," in his rude, posh, postprandial voice.

He was definitely having problems believing what he was seeing. He didn't know what to do; he looked beside himself. He was tapping his head as if I was a crazy foreign mother, and pointing his rifle at me, laughing all the while. He lowered his rifle and slapped his thighs again. He gestured for me to come into the building, into his office, the inner sanctum, a no-man's-land for would-be authors. "Oh, you'll invite me in now, will you, Mulqueeny? Well, it's too late to try to make up now, much too late. That was your big mistake."

It was a good time. I wanted to shout up to him: "Try rejecting this, arsehole."

Instead I adjusted the sights and raised my rifle too, laughing all the while. Then I stopped laughing, holding my breath, trying to keep the rifle steady, and put a bullet in his brain, right in the middle of his forehead. It looked to be the perfect shot, considering I'd done it so fast.

My little endomorphic friend stood in the window for a short while. He could have been calling out for Ms. Diane. I could see through the sights that he looked a little shocked, as if he'd been sobered up in double-quick time by a bucket of cold water being poured over his head. Or like a fish had been suddenly emptied out of a flower vase onto his lap. He was obviously now appreciating what a terrible mistake he'd made turning down my manuscript. There again, he may simply have been stunned by the view spread out before him. He took one step forward, as if to see it better, then crumpled beneath the windowsill. For a moment it appeared as if he was going to fall out of the window, but he didn't—not that it would have made much difference. It was perfect, apart from the fact that his death had been so quick. I wish it could have been a lingering one for the literary agent.

I stayed where I was for about ten minutes, watching and waiting for any signs of life—not from the man in the apartment block, who I knew was dead, but from anyone else. But there was nothing. The world was empty. Mortars flew overhead on their lonely trajectories, traveling from nowhere and disappearing into nowhere. Explosions and gunfire sounded distant. I sat and smoked a cigarette. I felt at peace in no-man's-land, at home, not in danger, sheltered beyond the realm of others, outside—from everyone, from both sides. I was quite alone.

I picked up my rifle and scratched an extra line on the butt. I reckoned I deserved 500 Deutsche Marks for shooting this one, this enemy, no doubt at all—probably more. And I thought to myself, "I'm a killer now, a real killer. I have no more time for art." I felt good, I felt very, very good. No one was going to laugh at me now. Ms. Diane was unlikely to snigger at the death of her boss, most unlikely. That would shut her up good and proper.

Later, I headed back to my own private aerie in the forest. I saw no one on my return journey, apart from the army truck driver who dropped me off on the Pale road without uttering one word on the whole trip. Mr. Stinky, however, buzzed a halfhearted welcome. Except for him, my brief sortie had gone, as far as I could tell, unnoticed.

Tonight, after I've finished writing in my notebook, I know I'll sleep like a baby. I will rest my head on my copy of *The Information*, and my head will be full of information.

I remember, when I was young, blowing up balloons. It must have been at Christmas, because I never had birthday parties, my father didn't believe in them—a waste of money, he said. Puff, puff, puff . . . The skin of the balloon was so tight, so stretched. Puff, puff, puff . . . Will it take any more air? Puff, puff . . . I remember thinking, if I blow one more time, it will burst. And I did—puff—a strong blow, and the balloon burst in my face.

I feel a little like that now. My head is like that balloon. It's very close to bursting. One more breath, one more puff, and perhaps I too will burst, my brains flying in every direction, my skull just shattered, empty fragments.

Why did I do it? I don't know. I have no idea. I couldn't give a satisfactory reply if someone asked me. Perhaps it was that perfectly motiveless act, without reason, which evolved out of nothing, owing its existence to no other occurrence. Perhaps I just wanted to clear the world of literary agents, especially bad ones. There again, let me argue, it could simply have been that I was being particularly creative, creating and acting out what might possibly make an interestingly dramatic scenario. Perhaps it was both. But to a degree it was premeditated, even though I hadn't thought about it in any great detail.

I returned to the Vraca camp two days later. A few of the men nodded, one even slapped me on the back. That's about as affectionate as these men can be. No one mentioned Santo. Maybe they don't know about him yet. I asked one or two people where he was, and they shrugged, indifferent. There was a new man in his bunk, but not in mine, which was strange—as if people sense these things.

I find it difficult writing in my journal now. It seems pointless, and requires too much effort.

It's early September. The weather's cooling down.

Yesterday, on the floor of the apartment I'm—not living in, but *existing* in—I found a broken mirror, smashed into many, many pieces. I picked up a shard and looked at the sliver of face I saw within it. I haven't seen myself for weeks, and was curious as to whether my appearance would be different in some way, reflecting the changes in my life.

I shave rarely nowadays, so there was a coarse growth around my lower face. The eyes stared out at me as if caught by surprise. My hair was uncombed, and made me look wild. I could have done with a wash. But I couldn't truly say that I looked very different, although there was something about the eyes. It was still "me" in the mirror, not someone new. It was the school janitor, the bloke who lived in the rundown sixties flat on Shoot Up Hill, the unrecognized scribe, the ex of Bridgette's. I think I'd hoped for, or expected, a noticeable change—although I'm not sure I know what I meant by that. I was disappointed that I appeared so normal, abnormally normal, and could only conclude that the mirror was lying, that it had decided to hide from me the fact that I was a different person.

Am I losing it? It's occurred to me that this could be the case. My grasp on reality is becoming more tenuous, it seems. Every action I go through is an imitation. I'm pretending. I'm one of the great pretenders. I do know that this, whatever it is, is what people do, this is how people behave, this is how they talk to each other, and smile or frown. When they do it, it's authentic, natural; but when I do it, it's not authentic, it's not genuine. I'm acting. I've always tried to behave like people expect me to, and say the things they expect me to say. Some of the time I take them in, fool my audience, and some of the time they can see right through me. I'm certainly never happy with my performance. I can see straight through it, the tricks and mannerisms, the pretence. I can't fool myself, it seems. I write it down, this reality, this life I'm now leading, in the hope it will become fiction, even turn into literature, but I know I could well be wasting my time. We're living in a postliterary world, as everyone's so keen to point out, and I'm just one of many picking over the corpse of the novel. By producing so many corpses myself, I'm closer to the action than most writers, of course, and that's surely no bad thing.

This morning I found myself standing at the apartment window. Such an innocuous statement, yet far from ordinary, about as far from everyday as one can possibly get in this far-from-everyday part of the world. I leant on the sill, and looked across to the hills on the other side of the city. I placed Mr. Gilhooley next to me. He has been a good companion for the past five or six months and I thought it appropriate, on such an occasion, that we were together. "It's time for us to leave, Gilhooley," I said to him. "Thank you for your company."

He wasn't too happy about this, I can tell you. "Can't you go by yourself?" he asked plaintively in his squeaky, unpleasant voice. "And aren't we a trifle exposed? Shouldn't we seek cover?" He was probably thinking fondly of my little cupboard under the stairs at school. Wouldn't he have liked to be hiding in there, with the janitor he so despised, right at that moment!

I rested my elbows on the sill. I didn't answer him. My rifle was propped up beside me. At first I was tense, which is normal when you're expecting a bullet to penetrate your brain, but soon I relaxed. I admit to keeping my eyes shut a lot of the time, as if not wanting to see what was heading my way, while I hummed some tune or other—I don't know what. I spoke a little to Mr. Gilhooley, but every time

I started a sentence, I wondered if I'd be given the opportunity to finish it. Happily, it was only small talk, primarily about his school, although I do also remember confessing to him about being plagued by feelings of mediocrity. I've been feeling discarded recently, as a person, son, and lover, but primarily as an author. Delete from records. Not wanted on voyage. Put outside with the garbage. It's not a pleasant feeling, even though I've renounced the writing profession. I'm about to die, I think, and I'm about to die with the knowledge that no one will remember me. Nor will anyone remember my books—how could they, when they haven't read them? When no one remembers you, you cease to exist, and that's a lonely thought. It makes me feel hollow. My life has amounted to nothing. Salieri achieved more than me, much more.

In October last year, about five months before I came to Sarajevo, the spacecraft *Magellan*, having mapped almost the whole of Venus, concluded its mission with a suicidal dive onto the surface of the planet. I could imagine the beeps, the static, the disembodied voices of NASA control, and then . . . and then . . . and then . . . the silence from the vastness of space. No more transmissions, no more information, just nothing—no thing.

All of this was going through my head, and I was telling Gilhooley about it. He, however, was not overly sympathetic when I told him of these doubts and fears, and said, in his smarmy schoolmasterly way, that he craved silence— "craved," for fuck's sake; who else could come up with a word like that? He told me to get a grip on myself or some such cliché.

I felt like Graham Greene playing Russian roulette when he was young. I wanted to die, I think that's what I wanted. Why else would I have done such a thing? It struck me as being a good idea at the time, it was as simple as that. Maybe

I was bored. But this is the astonishing thing: no one shot at me. Obviously I'd made a serious mistake killing the enemy sniper who'd been hunting me for so long. He'd never have missed an opportunity like this. I don't know what every sniper in the city was doing right then. Could they have all gone off for a tea break? I was annoyed: had I gone to all this trouble over the past few months to remain out of sight, and for no reason? Finally, after a good half-hour I straightened up, and was about to retreat from the window when there was an ear-shattering *crack!* and Mr. Gilhooley went flying backward across the room. I froze. I closed my eyes. My breathing was heavy, steady, as if I'd been in a deep sleep. Gilhooley was muttering and mumbling away on the floor behind me, but I ignored him. I waited, it seemed for an eternity, my eyes shut tight. And then it dawned on me: whoever was out there was not going to shoot me, not when I was presenting myself as a target. He wanted to hunt me. I decided to leave the window. Without hurrying, I picked Gilhooley up off the floor and retreated to the back of the room. The headmaster was complaining loudly about how this was the second or third time he'd been shot and yet I was still unscathed. "It's so unfair," he said, "the way you stick me out in the open, a lightning rod for all the world to see." I told him he'd scarcely been sympathetic to the fears and doubts I'd just been voicing, and that he should try to get a grip of himself and pull himself together. He stopped whimpering then, and sank into a quiet sulk. I wasn't sure I could be bothered to patch him up again.

I sat on the floor and lit a cigarette. My hands were shaking. I noticed that, but only after the event. I'd obviously decided there was little reason to live, but nor, as far as I could tell, was there much of a reason to die.

When I've finished writing this sentence, this sentence I'm writing now, I shall close this Collins notebook for the last time and throw it, along with its companion volume, if possible with a degree of nonchalance and urbanity, into the far corner of this room, where I'll leave them to rot or perhaps, you never know—and I truly don't care—to one day rise up, well up—even spew forth—on the tide of universal testimony.

And at the end, the very end, is the Word.

Acknowledgements

This novel has had a very long gestation, and many people have helped and encouraged me along the way. I thank them all, but in particular Barry Scott at Transit Lounge for his generosity and for being brave enough to go where no one else dared. Penelope Goodes for her professional, sensitive editing. Lindsay Barry for her patience in putting up with my dreams for far longer than anyone else. Merrin Cameron for her persistence in clearing so many blockages to publication. Dr. Leonie Naughton, my sometime muse, who sadly did not stay for the champagne. Bryan Keon-Cohen who is traveling the same path as me and always encourages. Most important, I wish to thank Elizabeth Orr, my favorite and most loyal reader, for her love and support, and for her endlessly perceptive, if frequently painful, criticisms.

An earlier version of *I Hate Martin Amis et al.* was the winner of the Victorian Premier's Literary Awards Prize for an Unpublished Manuscript.

About the Author

Peter Barry is an itinerant mongrel. He's English, French, Irish, and a Channel Islander. Born in England, he was brought up in Scotland. He has lived in Edinburgh, London, Paris, and Sydney, and he currently lives with his wife, and works as a copywriter, in Melbourne.